PLEA FOR PASSION

"Oh, do love me," she moaned. A shudder rippled through her. "Oh, love me, love me, love me…" He loosed her, and kissed each tremulous breast. He stretched up and kissed her lips, tongued her tongue, mouthed her neck, her perfumy ears. He lifted her in his arms, all of her, twisted her around. He held a warm foot in each hand, stroked the toes with their blood-dyed nails. He kissed the calves, the knees. He stroked the sensitive skin. Her raw nerves, crying for surcease, then broke her. "Mike, I can't stand it. Mike!" And she slapped him, beat her fist against his back and thews. "Ooh… ooh…" Her little fists pounded.

His blood roared like a cataract. He swung her, brought her down across his lap…

THE LUSTFUL THREE

TOM HARLAND

CUTTING EDGE

ISBN-13: 978-1-952138-95-9

Published by
Cutting Edge Books
PO Box 8212
Calabasas, CA 91372
www.cuttingedgebooks.com

CHAPTER ONE

IT WAS one of those infrequent hot July nights along the California coast. At Slat Landing, a commercial fishing boat chugged slowly down the narrow channel, her red and green running lights reflected in the back window of the old house built out over the fuel dock. In the stifling heat of the kitchen the card game stopped for a moment.

A leaky faucet dripped in the sink. Where some beer had been spilled, a fly crawled on the wet table. In shirtsleeves, old Jake Adam blinked, staring out through the window. He worked his toothless gums, muttering aimlessly about another boat coming in. Nobody answered him. His son, Ted, wiped his hand across his skinny face and looked around to where his wife stood languidly in the doorway between the living room and kitchen.

"Holly."

"What?"

"God damn it, listen to me."

"All right," she said sulkily. "What now?"

"Get Mike another drink."

Mike Shannon started to shake his head and then changed his mind. If the kid wanted to prove he was a big man by yelling at his wife, so let him. To hell with it. Mike waited. The old man told Ted to shuffle and deal and, while they went back to arguing over the cribbage board, Mike moved his chair away from the table. He glanced at Holly.

She looked right back at him. "Beer or whiskey?"

"Whiskey," Mike said, and a drum started pounding in his head. It would mean trouble, but her eyes said she was ready. Anything he wanted. Just ask. Anything. The drum hammered heat. Hunger burned hard in the pit of his stomach. Then she turned. The wide circle of her cotton dress swirled pink against her bare, tanned legs. High heels glittered. Coppery tints shimmered sleekly in her thick, blond ponytail. Her supple hips swayed as she walked, her back toward him. Mike suddenly thought nakedness, lovely slim nakedness. When she stopped at the refrigerator and glanced over her shoulder, he knew that she was reading his mind.

"Mike," she said, "How do you want it?"

How did he want it, he thought.

She stared right into his eyes. A trace of moisture glistened on the warm red curve of her mouth. Nineteen, going on twenty, Mike guessed. Not that age had anything to do with what she was offering.

He carefully kept his voice from betraying any emotion. "Just ice," he said. "No water."

She spoke slowly, huskily.

"Anything else?"

Double meaning? Honest to God, her mouth said one thing but there was no mistaking that another was in her mind. She wanted him to get the message.

Mike breathed sweltering stickiness. He had come only to talk to Jake about the fuel dock job. Holly was extra. Mike lit a cigarette and looked away from her. A litter of butts spilled over from the ash tray. The unshaded light over the table glittered on sweat, Ted's sweat, and all at once he looked up. "Hey, Mike. Watch."

Ted slapped down a card.

"Fifteen two and three in a row." He pegged the points. "Hell, man, how about that?" The boy squinted and picked up his bottle of beer. He swallowed. Then he rubbed his hands on his sweaty T-shirt. "Pretty good, huh?"

Mike stood up. "You're doing fine, Ted."

"Watch me cop it."

The kid was getting drunk. Mike knew the signs. And because he had been raised in Slat Landing himself, Mike knew all about Ted. Ted had always been considered a mean little bastard. More beer and he would start getting nasty. Maybe he would even razz Mike about quitting the ring. That was one thing Mike wanted to forget.

"I need some fresh air," Mike said.

"Sure," Ted smirked. "I forgot. You fighters have to keep healthy."

"That's over, Ted. I told you."

Mike kept his voice steady but his shoulders stiffened. Unconsciously, he moved a little, shifting his weight. One more smart crack, that was all it would take. He held his breath, but Ted only grinned.

"Okay, Mike." Ted blinked and licked his thin lips. "Look, if you want to talk some more about the job with Pa, don't let me or Holly stop you."

"I guess that's settled," Mike said.

The old man looked up. "I'm depending on you, Mike."

"Sure, Jake."

"The shack comfortable?"

"It will do."

"Well," Jake said, "I want you to be happy." He sniffled, his old voice rasping thinly. Light fringed his skimpy gray hair. "Of course, I can't equal the money you was making in the ring. But you told me you didn't come out so well, when you added it up."

"I came out broke," Mike said.

"Well," Jake said, "I'm glad you'll be working for me. I knew your Pa. I knew you before you was old enough to shave. By God, I can trust you and that's something these days. Mike, it ain't easy for an old man to run no damn fuel dock. And this will give you a chance to get on your feet."

"Sure, Jake. Thanks."

"I got Ted's college expenses to think about," Jake went on. "My back's still killin' me, too. I need another operation. But we might have a good fishing season around here this year. If we do, I'll see you get a raise. That's a promise."

"Fine," Mike said.

Jake sucked his cheeks, chewing his gums. The cords in his leathery neck worked like rawhide. His blue eyes watered. Rubbing his grease-gritted knuckles across his nose, he said, "Of course, with Ted and Holly coming down like this to stay the summer, I won't be able to help out as much as I like but you'll get paid for the extra work. And you'll get weekends off. Come Saturday, me or Ted will take over."

Mike nodded. Sixty-five a week and a shack. It sure as hell wasn't much, but there might be a dividend. He took a quick look at Holly. She had everything.

He lifted his cigarette and inhaled. Tobacco burned in his throat. The drum throbbed. One more woman. That was all he needed. Mike breathed the thought, smoke curling blue in the glare of the light. He turned and managed to get himself outside before Jake could start going over the whole thing again.

The porch creaked under Mike's weight. He went down the rickety steps to the fuel-dock mooring float. Around the rotting piling that supported the back porch, oily water gurgled sluggishly. Mike walked across the big wooden float to the back of the little office shack. He flipped his cigarette into the water. In the channel, the fishing boat chugged toward her berth at the head of the slough. Above the dock, past the house and the crumbling sardine canneries, a man and woman strolled unsteadily toward Blue Gull Tavern and the collection of straggling buildings that made up Slat Landing. The woman giggled. A tossed bottle splashed into the weedy shallows.

"Mike? Don't you want your drink?"

He looked up. Holly was standing at the head of the stairway.

"Sorry," Mike said. "I forgot."

He walked back to the ramp below the stairs and made a move to go up but Holly shook her head, started down with the glass. The pink dress fluttered. At the bottom of the stairs, she brushed against him. He helped her to the float and took the glass from her hand.

"Thanks, Holly."

"It was no trouble."

She looked up. Christ, it was like being hit. Time tipped. Heat choked in Mike's throat. The voices of Ted and old Jake bickering in the kitchen were sounds from another world. Reality was the catlike softness of Holly's greenish eyes, the sweet, musky woman-smell of her. Under the low neckline of her dress, the curving thrust of her breasts made shadows. In the hollow of her throat, her pulse throbbed. Night darkened the blond ponytail. And he could hear her saying it silently.

Anything.

Just ask me. I'll give you anything…

Mike tried to get hold of himself. He turned, setting the glass down on the bench behind the shack. Then, lifting his arm, he fumbled in the pocket of his khaki shirt for a cigarette. His lighter flickered. He inhaled.

"Mike, I like you."

Just like that. In the ring, during that last fight, facing the top contender, Mike had known the God-awful feeling of being in over his head. Now the feeling returned. Somewhere behind those hot, yielding eyes, she was ahead of him. He knew it. As on that night in the ring, he felt clumsy.

"You've got a husband," he said.

"I can still be lonely."

"You don't even know me, Holly."

"That doesn't matter."

"You're only a kid."

"I'm nineteen. I've been married more than a year."

"All right," Mike said. He took a deep drag from the cigarette. "So you're nineteen. Well, I'm twenty-five, and I've done a lot of living. Ted probably told you. I was real big for a while. I licked some good men. I got to believing I was great, not knowing the fix was on. Then I got beat, beat badly, the first time a classy opponent leveled against me. My bubble burst. The syndicate broke me. I crawled home looking for a little peace, a chance to lick my wounds—and the one thing I don't want is more trouble. And that's what you are. Trouble." Mike tossed his cigarette over the railing. "Hell," he finished bitterly, "I've got no business even talking to you."

"Why?"

"I just told you. Listen, old Jake had the decency to give me this job. I don't want to give him any grief."

"Over me?"

"Yes."

"But I want you to like me."

"Holly, for God's sake."

She moved closer. Under the dress she was sleek nakedness. She slipped her hand inside his shirt. The tips of her fingers trembled. Her legs moved.

"Mike, I don't see why we can't be friends."

He closed his hands over her wrists and forced down her arms. She put her head back. Shadows slanted along the planes of her cheeks. Light darkened her blond hair. A loud stumbling sound came from the house, and she shivered.

"Holly," Ted yelled.

"Yes, Ted."

"What the hell are you doing?"

"Just talking to Mike."

"Well, get the hell up here and find me and Pa some more beer."

Holly turned back to Mike. She stared into his eyes. Anything. Just ask me. She didn't have to put it into words. He knew. Anything and everything. Her lips parted.

"Mike," she whispered. "I'll be seeing you." Then, a§ Ted yelled again, she turned and started up the steps. "All right, darling," she called. "I'm coming."

CHAPTER TWO

BY DARK, a low fog had drifted in over the sand dunes. The lights of the Slat Landing Hotel blurred in the soft mist. A wet cat trotted across the dirt road and disappeared under the rotting foundation of one of the dilapidated canneries. In the Blue Gull Tavern, two fishermen and their fat, fortyish girlfriends hunched over a table in a booth by the window. Cigarette smoke made a bluish haze. The juke box belted out a hillbilly tune. At one end of the long bar, two truck drivers shook dice for drinks. Mig, the cocktail waitress, talked to Mike.

She was boyishly slim in black Capri pants. Her black sweater fitted snugly over her breasts. She had her hair done like an Italian movie star. And—he had to smile— it was dyed a bright orange.

"So you're home, Mike."

"Yes, Mig. I'm back."

"Working for old Jake, you say?"

Mike nodded, turning a little on the stool. He lit a cigarette. He had hardly known she was alive when he was in high school. It seemed a long time ago. She had been cute, then. Just look at her now. That outrageous orange hair. No wonder her marriage had ended in divorce. Even so, she couldn't be more than twenty-two or three. Too young to be making a freak out of herself. How did women think, anyway? He narrowed his eyes, looking her up and down. Maybe she would like being had. Maybe she wouldn't. A man never knew. He thought of Carla. A woman could pretend anything.

Mig said, "Well?"

"Well, what?"

"Do my charms pass inspection."

Mike grinned. "They're nice."

"I'm used to being stared at." Mig shrugged. "In here I get used to everything." She paused. "Didn't you graduate with Ted Adam?"

"Yes," Mike said.

"Skinny little runt," Mig said. "Stupid, too. The only way he'll ever get out of college is by flunking out, that's my guess. He's been attending classes three years, you know—or is it four?"

"I haven't kept check."

"He always gave me the creeps. That girl he married is a real knockout, though. Have you met Holly?" "Yes," Mike said. He turned, finishing his drink. He was thinking that Holly and Ted had gone back up to the city for a couple of days to pick up their things. The old man was running the fuel dock, and might be needing help. When Mig wanted to know what he thought of Holly, Mike shrugged. "She's a pretty kid."

"Nothing else?"

"No," Mike said. "Nothing else. Why?"

"Well," Mig replied softly, "last week when Ted was in, I heard him say he would kill any man who ever touches Holly."

"What's that got to do with me?"

"I don't know."

"I'm not worried," Mike said.

Mig leaned closer. Her lashes drooped with green mascara. The pale orange lipstick looked greasy. "How strange you are, Mike. You had the whole world on a string, then you lost it—but you don't seem to give a damn." A little smile touched her lips. "I'm sorry, Mike. Sometimes I talk too much."

"Forget it."

Mike was thinking: All right, so Holly isn't here. But Carla is.

Carla had called him from the hotel.

Someone up front hammered on a table and demanded service. Hank, the balding bartender, signaled to Mig. Mike watched her go, wondering why her husband had divorced her. Maybe she was frigid or something. He shrugged. One never knew.

Mike faced the door, stabbing out his cigarette. Suddenly he saw her. Carla.

She came in with that swift grace he remembered. Her dark hair was damp. Little drops of mist glittered in it like tiny diamonds. Her legs were still sleek and long. The narrow straps of her high heels accentuated the slenderness of her ankles. A green sheath hugged her hips. She gave the impression of height without being tall. She gave the impression of self-confidence, too. When Mike stood up to greet her, she smiled.

"Hello, Carla."

"It's been a long time, Mike."

"Was that any of my doing?"

"Please, Mike, don't be bitter."

He shrugged and offered her a cigarette. She took the stool next to him. Tight and smooth, the dress clung to her knee. The men at the bar were staring at her, and a couple of the women, too, but she pretended not to notice. When Mike thumbed his lighter, she tilted her face to catch the flame.

Mike's hands were shaking. He thought back to the days when he had been Mike Shannon, the coming champion. Everything had glittered then. Fat Joe Nicca, his manager, had introduced Mike to Carla. She had been part of the glitter—along with the big money, the plush hotels, the expensive nightclubs: but she had been part of the bad times, too. Mike could still hear Joe Nicca saying, "Tell him, Carla. Tell him it was good while it lasted, but it's all over. Tell him why I brought you down here, Carla. Tell him you sell it."

Mike lifted his glass, gulped whiskey.

"Mike, aren't you going to buy me a drink?"

"Sorry."

He lifted a hand to get the bartender's attention. As they sat and sipped, Carla did the talking. Since his last big fight, six months before, she had been living mostly in New York, she told him.

"I missed you, Mike."

"Sure."

"I called every bar in town, trying to locate you. I'm glad I reached you here."

He grunted.

"You don't seem surprised to see me."

"I'm not." Mike swallowed the last of his drink. "A San Francisco paper ran the story last Sunday. The sports staff is getting together a series on professional boxing— they intend to blow the lid right off, and they have the blessing of the church people, state authorities, and a couple of Congressmen. And I'm among the fighters, they announced, that their reporters will talk to first—" Mike laughed grimly. "I figured Fat Joe might have seen the Sunday sports pages. I was pretty sure he would send somebody down to see me."

"Mike," Carla whispered. "Fat Joe has nothing to do with my coming here. I came because I had to see you again. Can't you believe me?"

"No," he said. "Why should I have any faith in you? Why should I have faith in anybody?"

She was about to answer when one of the truck jockeys at the bar, who had been staring at Mike, unexpectedly spoke:

"So you're Shannon!"

Mike turned. The trucker, stocky, wide across the shoulders, rubbed his fist across his chin and moved toward Mike.

"You're the fighter, right?"

"I was," Mike growled.

"You ever get beat?"

"What's it to you?"

The truck driver grinned, sent a wink at his buddy, then boldly eyed Carla.

"Nice," he said softly. He glanced at Mike. "Who's your girl friend?"

Mike crushed out his cigarette. Except for the moaning of the juke box, the tavern was silent. Everybody was looking at him. Hell, he had expected something of the sort, sooner or later. In six months of drifting, he had run into a number of tough guys out to make a rep. They all wanted a chance to boast that they had knocked down the man who had nearly fought himself into a bout with the champion. Mike felt a hard knot of hate in his guts. These cheap bar-fighters …

"Look," the truck driver said, "I asked you a question. Did you hear me?"

Mike stood up.

"I heard you," he said. He paused and then very quietly he added, "Why don't you go back and sit down. Don't press your luck."

"You think I'm scared of you?"

"No," Mike said.

"All right," the truck driver said smugly. "We'll take it from the start. Who's your girl friend?"

"Go choke yourself," Mike said, and turned his back.

Carla squealed when the clubbing fist swung viciously at Mike's head. At the sound, Mike moved, and the blow glanced off his shoulder. He wheeled. Now it was his turn. He threw a straight left. The stocky driver, blood smearing his mouth, staggered back against the juke box. His head sagged, and he went down to his knees. He gulped for breath.

Finally, rubbing his hand across his cut lip, he growled, "Damn you, Shannon. You never gave me a chance."

"Have it your way," Mike said. "I told you to lay off."

It ended there. The two truck men marched out. The bartender set up a round of drinks. Everyone was staring at Mike.

"Carla," he said, "let's get out of here."

They pushed their way through the crowd. Outside, the wind caught the skirt of her dress and flattened it against her sleek legs. Fog moved mistily. On the way over to the hotel, she clung to Mike's arm. She remarked that she had a bottle in her room. That sounded interesting to Mike and, upstairs, after he had mixed a pair of drinks, she slipped into his arms. The shades were drawn, the door locked. Eternity was the hot curve of her mouth. Mike kissed it.

"I love you, Mike."

"Sure."

"I always loved you."

Sure. Mike knew. She was his very own whore. Love by the numbers. He laughed. Then she told him that he still looked fast and solid, that he could still go back to fighting. But he shut her up.

"I don't want to remember."

"All right," she whispered. "You don't have to remember that. Just remember me. Mike, I've been so lonely."

"Did Fat Joe tell you to say that?"

"Don't try to hurt me, Mike."

She turned out the light. A soft glow reflected through the window blinds from the street lamps below.

Mike's thoughts raced. He could have her if he wanted her. All he had to do was say the word. Assembly line seduction. So much whiskey. So many lies. Not money, though, not this time. Carla knew he had no money.

"Mike, I love you."

He took his cue.

"It's too late, Carla."

"It's never too late."

She twisted free of his hands. Expertly, she wriggled out of her dress. It dropped to the floor. She turned gracefully, supple shadows rippling nakedness. On the bed, her dark hair flared loosely. Her breath came quickly. She lifted her hands, fumbling, stripping. Her fingers pushed hot. He kissed her mouth.

He whispered her name. He caressed her. And he thought: Mike, the great lover? Oh, no, I'm not drunk enough to believe that. But go on, Carla, whimper. Pretend. Moan. What the hell, I've been through the mill. I don't expect stardust.

"Mike, please believe me. I love you." She trembled. Her arms went around his neck. Her lips burned hungrily. The tip of her tongue touched fire. The taut clinging yielded and suddenly her warmth melted him. He closed his fists in her hair.

But he knew he should have been back at the dock, helping old Jake...

CHAPTER THREE

EARLY MONDAY, Mike got out in the hot sun to hose down the fuel dock. The smell of coffee drifted out of the shack, where he had left the pot on the little electric plate. Water sluiced, streamed over the side of the mooring float. On the road above, passing in front of the house, a truck loaded with iced salmon jolted toward the highway bridge. He glanced after it, then gazed across the slough at a small day boat backing away from a rickety wharf, her orange trim glistening. In the stern well, a short but brawny Italian fisherman named Geeko cut bait for cod lines. He waved to Mike. Sea gulls squawked, wheeling, swooping to snatch the bait scraps from the water.

Minutes later, a big northern troller moored to fuel. She took six hundred gallons. A gangling tow-headed kid, working on a wad of tobacco, kept spitting over the side. When the tanks were finally topped off, the skipper, a heavy-shouldered Norwegian, signed the bill. Before an hour had passed, two smaller boats had stopped at the dock. Then old Jake came down from the house.

Humping and wheezing, clad in baggy old khakis and a dirty denim shirt, Jake looked more like a skidrow bum than the owner of valuable real estate. Reaching the foot of the steps, he mopped his face with a tattered bandanna.

"Hot."

"Yeah, Jake."

"Been pretty busy?"

Mike was sure the old snoop had come to pry. Where there was money involved, he meant to know what was going on.

"Eight hundred forty gallons," said Mike.

Jake scratched a match on the "no smoking" sign and lit his pipe. At the first puff, he coughed as though about to choke to death. His rheumy eyes watered as he puffed again. After a third puff, he muttered with gloomy satisfaction, "It keeps a person hopping."

"Sure does, Jake."

"There's a hell of a lot of expense and overhead in a business like this. God damn, with taxes so high, it ain't hardly worth the effort."

"Too bad Ted can't help you out."

"He's got studying to do. I want him to amount to something." The old man paused and squinted. "I hear tell you had a fight Saturday at the Blue Gull."

"Sort of an argument, Jake."

"I talked to Hank, the bartender. He says you hit that fellow hard." Jake smoked thoughtfully. "Hank says a girl was with you. Friend of yours?"

"Sort of," Mike said.

"You ain't figuring on leaving me, are you? To go back to prize fighting?"

"No, Jake. I'm finished with that."

"I can't understand why you didn't come out with a pile of money."

"Somebody did, Jake. I didn't. When I got back here I was broke. I told you that."

Jake nodded. "Hank said this girl looked like one of them models. One of them Hollywood girls, maybe." He waited, sucking his pipe. When Mike did not answer, Jake said, "I'll tell you something, Mike. If things pick up, you'll get a raise. After Ted goes back to college in the fall."

"Okay, Jake."

"I don't want you quitting on me."

"I'm not figuring on quitting. Don't worry about it."

The old man talked on a while, grumbling about taxes, low profits, expenses. Finally he announced that he had to go into town, and he stomped toward the old panel truck parked below the steep driveway.

Mike handled a little flurry of business, then managed to find time to shave and change into a clean shirt. He was warming up the coffee when Holly came down to the dock.

She looked as if she had just showered. Her pale-blue shorts and matching halter were immaculate. The clean lines of her slender legs, the little naked slap of her sandals on the dock boards, these brought a catch to his throat. The ponytail shimmered in the seabreeze. She gazed at him openly. Candidly.

No pretending. No dollar sign.

The drum started to beat.

Anything.

Just ask me.

"Hi," she said.

Mike forced a grin. What the hell was she doing to him? He had had plenty of women. A woman was only a woman. Holly had nothing that Carla did not have. Don't be a chump, he thought. This is Ted's wife. He took a deep breath.

"Hello, Holly."

He said her name easily, keeping his voice steady; but his heart tripped as she came nearer. The movement of her hips was an invitation, surely. Yet there remained something elusive about her, something withheld despite her unspoken promises. *Anything. Anything at all.* She was a temptress, and at the same time still a child. That was it, he decided. That was the contradiction in her.

"Well," she said. "It's nice to be back."

"Did you have a good trip?'

"With Ted? Are you kidding?"

"He's your husband."

She smiled. Under the blue halter, the satiny curves of her breasts breathed tightly.

"So?" she said.

Mike lit a cigarette. Those breasts, he thought. Those lonely, swelling breasts.

"Pa told me about your fight. Who was the lucky girl?"

"An old friend of mine from L.A."

"That's nice." The satiny breasts rose and fell a little faster. "He said you spent the night at the hotel. At least, somebody told him you did."

"What's it to you?"

"It might not be anything, Mike." She paused. "What's the girl's name?"

"Carla."

"She a good friend?"

"We were engaged."

"It broke up?"

"Yes."

"She must have been crazy to break off with you, Mike."

Mike shrugged.

"I had nothing to offer after I lost my big fight."

"You'd always have something to offer." She smiled. "I know you think I shouldn't be talking so frankly."

"You've got a husband."

"Stop reminding me." Holly shrugged. "Oh, hell," she said suddenly. "Let's talk about something else. Ask me in for a cup of coffee."

"I'm not so sure I should."

"Please, Mike."

"All right." He walked her to the door of the shack. She brushed against him. In the channel, passing the dock, a drag boat turned at the buoy. The mutter of diesel exhaust muted in with the hammering beat of Mike's heart. Wanting twisted down in him, down to his loins. You dumb bastard, he thought, stop it. But aloud, he got over the moment by apologizing for the unmade bunk and the dirty frying pan on the hot plate. "I've been too busy to clean up."

"That's all right. I'll come in later and straighten out the place."

She sat down on the edge of the bunk. Mike poured coffee. She balanced the cup on her knee and leaned against the desk. It had been built high to be worked at standing. The edge of it cut across her back. Light glinted in Holly's hair and curved with the warm turn of her tanned leg. She lifted the cup and drank but then, before either of them could pick up the threads of conversation, footfalls sounded on the dock and Ted stuck his head through the open doorway.

Mike set his cup on the desk and stood up straight. He was surprised when Ted barely glanced at Holly, and said mildly, "I'm looking for my father. Seen him anywhere?"

"He was down here," Mike said. "I think he drove into town."

"How long ago?"

"Must be more than an hour now."

"Damn it. Probably he'll be gone all day." Ted glanced at Holly again. "I need some money."

"Who has money?"

"Listen, you blond bitch," Ted snapped, "don't get wise with me."

"All right, Ted."

"By God, it better be all right."

"Well," Holly said patiently. "I really can't help you, Ted. You know I don't have any cash."

Ted wiped his hand across his face. He muttered that he needed a drink, and then he found a pencil and a scrap of paper. Leaning over the desk, he wrote out an I.O.U. for twenty dollars and then handed the piece of paper to Mike.

"You give me the money and put that in the cash register. I'll tell Pa." Ted paused, blinking. "Well, hurry up," he said nastily. "Just because you pushed some drunk truck driver around up at the Blue Gull, that doesn't make you champion of the world."

"Relax, Ted."

"Well, give me the money."

Mike hesitated, rage flaming. Then, getting hold of himself, deciding he didn't care one way or the other, he punched the register. He shoved Ted's chit into the cash drawer and gave him a ten, a five and five ones. Ted jammed the money into his pocket and said he was going up to the Blue Gull.

"I won't be long."

"Okay. I hope this is all right with Jake."

"You let me do the worrying."

Mike kept his temper under control, fighting down the urge to smack Ted. It would do no good. There had to be a time when he would quit solving problems with his fists. This was as good a time as any. Mike managed a grin and, finally, after Ted had left, turning back to Holly, Mike let the anger drain away.

"I guess I'm lucky," he said.

"Why?"

"I figured he might be sore about you being down here."

"All he ever worries about is a bottle of booze."

"That's hard to believe."

"It's true."

Holly got up. She walked to where Mike stood by the desk. She looked at him. Her mouth was warm and red. She parted her lips. If Ted craved only booze, he must be out of his mind, thought Mike, feeling the press of her leg.

"I don't want to talk about Ted," said Holly.

"What do you want?"

"Mike," she whispered, "don't you know?"

"Yes," he said. "I guess I do." He pulled her to him. Heat flamed hard in his stomach.

Her mouth was hot. The slim yielding was a kind of begging; the warm melting breath of surrender was a pleading.

But when he responded, when he lifted Holly in his arms and started for the bunk, she whispered into his ear, "Not now, Mike."

He set her down, his blood racing.

"I'd best get into the house," she said.

"Don't go, Holly." He was beyond caution, beyond calculation.

"I've got to."

"Why?"

"Ted is liable to be back, or Pa. Anyway, Mike, it's broad daylight. This isn't the time."

"When?"

"Later, Mike."

"Tonight?"

"Yes, Mike. If I can."

"Promise?"

"Mike, you don't need to doubt me."

He kissed her. The damp, perfumed curve of her mouth trembled against his lips. No, he didn't need to doubt her. She wanted what he wanted. Desire guided the pleading tip of her tongue. In the breathlessness of that last throaty whisper, she had belonged to him. Her eyes had pooled nakedness.

She backed out of his embrace, turned and fled out of the shack.

CHAPTER FOUR

MIKE COUNTED time crazily. Holly. Holly! God, she wanted to give. There was nothing halfway. Anything. He had been right from the beginning.

Anything.

Just ask me.

The words pounded. Mike smoked a cigarette. Tobacco tasted hot. Across the slough, sun glared. Mike squinted. Once, he told himself—once in a lifetime, if you were lucky, you might have a girl like Holly come along. He breathed the oil smell and flipped his cigarette into the water. Above, on the road, a truck rattled under a load of empty fish boxes. Down the channel, at the cannery wharf, the ice machine whined, spewing crushed ice down a pipe-sized hose and into the hold of a trolling boat. A gang of Mexicans came down the bank to fish. A tug puffed past.

An hour or so after that, just as Mike finished pumping fuel into a bait boat, Ted returned to the float. He had had a few drinks and was carrying a bottle.

"Pa back?"

"No," Mike said.

"I'll level with you. He'll be sore because you gave me money out of the cash register." He sat down, propping his back against the shack. He opened his bottle.

"How about a drink, Mike?"

"No, thanks."

"Suit yourself." Ted tipped the bottle. He swallowed and then, after wiping his mouth with the palm of his hand, he put the cap back on. "Goes down like silk."

"Keep drinking," Mike said, "and they'll be wrapping you in silk. Black silk."

"You mean a shroud?"

"That's right, Ted."

"I guess you think that's pretty funny."

"No. I'm just telling you. Do many of you college kids drink like that?"

"I'm no college kid."

Ted got out his cigarettes. He lit one and inhaled deeply. Holding the cigarette between his thumb and his tobacco-stained forefinger, he studied the water thoughtfully. Finally, he spoke.

"I guess you've had experience."

"Doing what?"

"Drinking."

"Yes," Mike said. "I hit the bottle pretty hard for a while."

"After you quit the ring?"

"I didn't quit, Ted. I got beat."

"I guess you still think it makes you a hero."

"No." Mike took a deep breath. "It was no good, Ted. I know that now. It was just a big bubble. They built me up. When they had everything arranged the way they wanted it, they lowered the boom. I never had a chance. I thought I did, but I didn't."

"So you came home."

"Yeah, Ted. I came home."

Ted blinked. He uncapped the bottle and took another drink. "Maybe you think you got troubles," he said. "Well, I got worse ones." He did not elaborate. But suddenly he blurted that he had seen Carla at the hotel coffee-shop. She had been pointed out to him as the girl Mike had fought over in the bar. "God damn," Ted said. "I didn't know you had something that good stashed away." Ted grinned and licked his lips. "Maybe that's what I need."

"You've got a wife."

"That little bitch?" Ted puffed jerkily at his cigarette. "There's a lot you don't know."

"I guess so."

"You're damned right. I could tell you a whole lot. Do you know the property my old man owns here at Slat Landing is worth a hundred thousand dollars?"

"No," Mike said. "I didn't know that."

"Well," Ted said. "Neither did I until just recently. It was she who told me. Little old Holly knows those things. You bet. Right behind her sweet blue eyes, she's got a damned adding machine. You know those old company houses they built up the river when they were canning sardines? Well, she was living up there with one of her father's sisters when I started going with her. A real sweet little blond high-school kid." Ted nodded, muttering to himself and then, talking to Mike again, said, "Hell, you've seen her. Any guy could go for that. Anyway, her aunt was going back to Ohio and so I married Holly. Yes, sir—I married her. But let me tell you something. She had it all figured from the start. My old man has got more money than he knows about. One of these days I stand to get it. Two and two make four. Just ask Holly. She's got all the answers tucked away. You know how she spells love, Mike?"

"No."

"M-o-n-e-y."

"Is that right?"

"Know something else?"

"You're drinking too much."

"No," Ted said. "I'm not drinking too much and I don't need any punchy fighter telling me my business, either." Ted dropped his cigarette. It smoldered on the oil-stained planking. When Mike walked over to kick it into the water, Ted grinned.

"Let the damned place burn down."

"You wouldn't care?"

"Hell, no. Holly would though. It's all money. She figures to get her hands on every dime, sooner or later." Ted paused and then voiced what was still on his mind. "That Carla is quite a girl."

"She's pretty."

"Sure," Ted said. "All over, I'll bet." He squinted up at Mike. "Who is she?"

"An old friend of mine. We broke up."

"You were up at the hotel with her so you're still getting your share, right?"

"Why don't you ask Carla?"

"Maybe I will." Ted rubbed his mouth. "As soon as I get a little time."

"Well," Mike said. "You'd better hurry. I've got a hunch she'll be leaving."

"That ain't what she told me."

"You spoke to her?"

"We exchanged a few words." Ted laughed. "She said she'd be here for most of the summer. I got the feeling she figured you would be making up with her. I got the feeling she expects you to be squiring her around." "Don't count on it."

"Suits me," Ted said. "If you haven't got it staked out, I'd like to get a little of it myself."

"How about Holly?"

"I'll do the worrying about her." Ted took off the cap and tipped up the bottle. Sunlight glittered on brown glass. Ted's throat worked. A trickle of whiskey spilled down his chin. He capped the bottle and pulled his forearm across his face. Then, staring at Mike, Ted repeated himself. "I'll do the worrying about her." He paused. "Yes, sir," he mumbled, "she's mine. I'll tell you one more thing, Mike. If I ever have any more trouble with her, I'm going to knock her brains out."

"You don't mean that, Ted."

"Yes," Ted muttered. "I mean it."

He staggered up and stuck his bottle inside his shirt, for a boat was swinging in from the channel to moor and take fuel. By the time Mike was free again, Ted had gone back up the steps toward the house. Then, less than a half-hour later, the old man came down to the dock.

"How you doing, Mike?"

"Just fine, Jake."

Jake scratched his dirty fingers through thin gray hair. He coughed and spit over the side of the float.

"I guess Ted was down here."

"Yes," Mike said.

"That's what Holly told me." Jake sniffled, rubbing his fist back and forth across his nose. "She said he got some money from you."

"He gave me an I.O.U. for it, Jake."

"How much?"

"Twenty dollars."

"Well," Jake sighed. "I can't tell you not to do it, Mike. Ted is my boy. Ever since he got married and tried to keep on going to school at the same time, he's been trying to do too much. He's got a mind. He's got a nice little wife, too. Of course, I can't hardly afford to spend all I'm spending but a man has got to do what he can. It's nice for me to have him and Holly down here, you know. When they are up in the city where Ted goes to school, I hardly see 'em. A man my age gets lonely. I'll talk to Ted, though."

"You're not sore at me?"

"Hell, no. Ted is my boy."

"How about the next time?"

"I'll talk to Holly."

Mike said, "I may as well tell you Ted is—uh—drinking a little."

"Drunk?"

"Headed that way, Jake."

The old man blinked his eyes. "I don't understand him. Do you, Mike?"

"He's your boy, Jake."

"You went to school with him, Mike."

"He's still your boy."

"Well, I don't know, Mike. Maybe he's studying too much. I don't know a lot about things like college, but I do know he's got a wonderful little girl for a wife. So why should he drink?"

"That's a good question, Jake."

"She loves him."

"Sure, Jake." Mike kept a straight face.

After talking back and forth for a few more minutes, the old man climbed the steps, content to leave Mike in possession of the fuel dock.

For the rest of the day, Mike worked alone. At noon, he opened a can of soup and made himself another pot of coffee. At five-thirty he locked up and left a note on the door saying he would be back in an hour. He walked up to eat at the hamburger joint next to the hotel. The food was pretty bad but he did not want to take a chance on meeting Carla in the coffee shop. He did not want to risk another brawl in the Blue Gull, either. So instead of going in there after he had eaten, Mike picked up a fifth at the store.

Going back, he heard Jake and Ted arguing in the kitchen but Mike did not stop. He went back down to the float. He had another little flurry of business before dark, then along about eight-thirty the harbor quieted down. Occasionally an incoming boat chugged past the dock but finally Mike turned out the dock lights. He stripped, and took a bath. The shower was fixed to the outside of the shack under a canvas shelter. Mike toweled dry and changed into clean khakis. He mixed a drink. The clock over the desk said ten to nine and it was just an hour later when Holly walked in without knocking.

"Mike."

"You came."

"Yes," she whispered. "Why are you surprised?"

He closed the door. She was wearing high heels but her legs were bare. Through her ligh cotton dress, his hands felt nakedness. She looked up. Her lipstick glistened. The neckline of the dress breathed tightly over the warm satiny curves of her breasts. She pressed against him. Her hips moved and she lifted her hands, touching his cheeks with the tips of her fingers. He bent down. His lips brushed over her mouth. She caught her breath.

"Mike."

"Yes."

"Undress me."

"You're not afraid?"

"No."

"What about Ted?"

"He passed out. Dead-drunk."

"Jake?"

"Sound asleep."

"It's just you and me, Holly."

"Yes, Mike," she whispered. "We're the only ones in the world."

Her lips parted and with the click of the lock, with darkness except for a streak of moonlight slanting the shaded window, she yielded hungrily to his hands. Nakedly, her golden hair loose, flared soft against the bunk pillow, she moved her hands over his bare shoulders. She turned, girlish softness crushing him. He kissed her silkily, sliding his hands down the sleekness of her back. Her tongue burned. Her body was like a taut bow, yet soft, soft...

"Mike, I love you."

"You can't know that. We just met."

"I know I love you," she whispered savagely. "Love is something that doesn't need time. It needs only itself." She shivered.

"Oh, God, Mike. Hold me tight." A moan trembled on her mouth. She pushed her hands up and closed her fingers in his hair. Then once more, her voice shuddering breathlessly, she begged with his name. "Mike. Mike. I love you. Please, Mike. Say you love me."

"I love you."

"Do you mean it?"

"Yes," Mike said. He tightened his arms. "I mean it. I mean it now." He yielded then to wonder and lust. Shaking with passion, he bent and kissed the delectable breasts, each in turn. The pink nipples greeted his tongue. His hands possessed the round, lithe hips of Holly. His thews met her loins and her long legs spread and thrashed.

Then it was lips to lips, thigh to thigh, hard stomach to soft. Wet, clinging womanhood enveloped him, soaring him to furious heights. He plunged into electric ecstasy, shook and shattered with the unbearable bliss of it, until in shared detonation his soul spewed in unity with hers.

This was more than mating, he thought.

It was exaltation. It was joy so pure that it cut like agony.

CHAPTER FIVE

DURING THE NEXT ten days, Mike managed to be alone with Holly only twice. For one thing, old Jake took sick unexpectedly, and Holly devoted most of her time to nursing him. For another, Ted turned nasty. Once, when he came on Holly drinking coffee with Mike in the shack, he took a swing at Mike.

Why had Ted suddenly become suspicious? Had somebody been talking to him? By the next day, he was back to his drinking, the fight forgotten, but for a while Mike avoided being alone with Holly.

Ted spent a lot of time around the Blue Gull with Carla. It could be she had developed some interest in him; it could also be that she was trying to make Ted jealous, deliberately hinting that she had reason to believe an intimacy was developing between Mike and Holly. But on Tuesday of the second week, when Mike walked up to the hotel to talk to her, Carla just shrugged his questions aside.

"Mike," she said. "I don't care about Ted. He's just a tiresome little drunk. I'm staying here only because of you. Please believe me. You're the only man in my life."

"Did Fat Joe tell you to say that, too?"

"Mike, why should he be interested in what I do, except when he's got some job for me?"

"I suppose he doesn't care if I talk to those San Francisco reporters."

"Of course he cares."

"Did he send you up here to find out if I was going to spill what I know?"

"Mike, I would have come anyway."

"Okay, have it your way. But damn it, stop feeding Ted lies about me and Holly."

"Are they lies?"

That was as far as Mike got. She said they could talk more about it later but he did not kid himself. She knew. She had figured it out for herself, gathered it from what came over him when he mentioned Holly's name. All she had to do was keep Ted jealous and there was bound to be trouble. Christ, he figured he had stopped caring one way or the other about trouble but, at the end of the week, on Friday morning, he found out he was wrong.

Old Jake was well enough to take a turn outside that morning. Mike went up to make out an order for fuel to be phoned to the distributor. Jake stood in the driveway, talking over the order with Mike when Ted and Holly appeared, bound for the garage. They were driving over to Monterey for the day. Ted had already been drinking. When Holly said good morning to Mike, Ted whirled around.

"You bitch, get in the car."

"Ted, for God's sakes."

Ted yelled, "You keep your mouth shut, Holly, or I'll smack you senseless." He turned to glare at Mike. "I suppose you want to make something out of that?"

Mike took a deep breath. "No, Ted."

"Damn it, you're yellow."

"Have it your way."

"I suppose you'd like to take a swing at me?"

"No."

Ted spat on the ground and then lit a cigarette. When old Jake spoke to him, Ted told his father to go to hell.

"Stay out of my business. I'm not so damned dumb. Mike and Holly aren't fooling me." Ted inhaled angrily and then, his mouth splitting in a nasty grin, he started talking about Carla. "Maybe she's your chick, Mike. But what would you say," he asked, "if I told you I'd got some of that?"

"Easy, Ted."

"You think I'm lying?"

"It doesn't matter."

"The hell it doesn't. You think you're somebody special. Well, let me tell you something. I can make out, too. Think that over. She may be your girl but I can get it any time I want."

"That's fine, Ted."

"You don't believe me?"

"I told you it doesn't matter."

Ted cursed. "You're not fooling me, Mike. You care. You bastard, acting so damned quiet. Well, I know you hate my guts. You'd like to get me. Then you'd have Holly and Carla both. Well, nobody is getting me and if I ever catch you around my wife I'll fix you so you won't be breathing."

Mike held his temper. Finally, after dropping his cigarette and grinding it out on the sand, Ted backed his red convertible out of the garage. He roared the motor and spun the wheels. Dust kicked up. The glare of the sun gleamed red. At the turn, the convertible skidded around a truck. A horn blared and then Ted streaked across the bridge and out of sight.

"Mike," old Jake said. "I don't know what gets into that boy."

"That's all right."

"But that Holly—she's a fine girl."

"Sure she is."

"Maybe," the old man said, "Ted has been studying too hard. College ain't easy." He paused, staring down at the ground. "I wouldn't want no trouble around here."

"Don't worry, Jake."

Mike wanted to drop it there. He was sick of Ted. The kid was asking for a punch in the mouth. At the same time, Mike was aware that no matter what happened, he would not be able to get Holly out of his mind or his blood.

He went down to the shack. Home, he thought bitterly. All he had wanted was to settle down, to forget, but life did not stop just because he had been mauled in the prize ring. Now he wanted more, needed more. Holly.

Was it that bad? After all, couldn't he do without her? Could any woman be everything? He worked, trying to figure that out, but after a while Jake joined him on the fuel dock to help.

Jake puttered around until after dark that night.

For a long time, in spite of Mike's efforts to change the subject, Jake kept on talking about Ted and Holly but at last, in the late afternoon, he got off on how bad his stomach had been while he had been sick. He said he had intended to go to a doctor but Holly had told him it would be a waste of money. That got him going on how hard it was to make a dollar. He grumbled as though he were broke instead of being worth a hundred thousand dollars. He complained about the prices he had to pay at the stores and muttered that the government taxed a man until it wasn't worth owning property or trying to run a business. Then, after wearing that subject out, he got to reminiscing about the old days in Slat Landing. A little later, he started on Mike's career as a prize fighter.

"I guess," he kept saying, "You had some pretty high living."

By that time Mike was locking up, getting ready to change out of his working clothes; he just grunted, but Jake went right ahead anyway. He got up on the high stool in the shack, hunching back against the desk, puffing his pipe while Mike shaved.

"I guess you come by it natural."

"What, Jake?"

"Fighting."

Jake squinted. Under the raw bulb and the brim of his old hat, his thin face was sunken and wrinkled. He smoked thoughtfully, gumming the stem of his pipe.

"Yes," he went on, "you come by it natural. I remember your Pa. He was one hell of a fisherman. Weather didn't mean anything to him. If there was fish to be caught, he went out and got them. In a fight, he was just the same. Size didn't bother him a damn bit. He'd as soon fight a big man as a little man. I guess, being you was so small when she died, you don't remember your mother much. I do. She was as quick as light sand with that French dark hair. She could handle your Pa but once she was gone he didn't give a hoot in hell for anything. I told him he was drinking himself to death. He said that suited him fine. I know, before it was over, he lost everything and ended up being no more than a drunk around here but even if that's the way you remember him, Mike, he was a hard man in his day."

"It doesn't matter now, Jake. I grew up. I learned to get by on my own."

"Sure you did." Jake studied his pipe. "Maybe that made you tough. Anyhow," he said, "at least you made some money out of fighting."

"I never was good enough, Jake."

"That ain't what the papers said."

"I know," Mike said softly.

He finished shaving and wiped his face. No bad scars. He was lucky. It could have been a lot worse. He looked like a tough customer but at least his brains were not scrambled. The mirror glittered and, for a moment, while he stared mockingly at himself, the beginning came back.

He had been working at the time on a tuna clipper out of San Pedro. A national magazine doing an article on amateur boxing had sent a photographer to get some shots of him on the boat. The tough, young fisherman. Because he was good-looking, the spread had attracted some notice. A movie company got a little cheap publicity by letting out that they were considering a contract. Nothing had come of that, but while Mike was still riding the crest, Joe Nicca had come along.

Joe fronted for a syndicate of New York and Nevada gamblers. He had found Mike had turned in some surprising performances in the Golden Gloves and had tabbed Mike a natural. All it would take was a little training, he had told Mike. God, when you want to, you can believe everything or anything. Besides, Mike remembered bitterly, they had made it easy to believe.

A string of fixed fights. He should have guessed. Nobody gets to be an overnight sensation without somebody pulling the strings. There were too many angles to the fight game, too much that was rigged and arranged. Well, he hadn't guessed, chiefly because he had not been altogether bad, and could have licked some of those fighters on his own. His hands were naturally quick. In training he had swiftly learned balance, the trick of getting his weight into a punch. Boxing had come without any strain. His left jab had a sting. He looked good on TV. Yet it would have been better if he had been handed a real loss right at the start.

In that case, there would have been no big build-up but no big let-down, either.

Mike turned from the mirror and, tossing the towel on his bunk, reached for a clean shirt. To hell with it. He had been outclassed in the end, outsmarted, outboxed and beaten by one hell of a good fighter. The contender hadn't needed any fixes. His fists packed all the fixing required. Mike still tasted the hard smashes to the mouth, the jolting body blows. He could smell the heat and sweat, hear the roar of the crowd and feel the world exploding when he hit the canvas for the last time. The count came back: *eight, nine, ten…*

Mike said none of this to old Jake. What would be the use?

He turned his back on Jake. He climbed the steps, trudged toward the Blue Gull.

Carla was waiting there.

"Hi, darling."

He could not avoid her. Besides, in that first moment, as she always did, she made him aware of how lovely she was. Slim, her legs sleek in sheer nylons, her black dress molded to her slender figure, the high white collar at her throat giving her an oddly wicked virginal look, she watched him as he slid in next to her.

"Hello, Carla."

Without wanting to, Mike felt a hot surge of response to her. He saw the old wicked promise in her eyes. Light darkened in her hair, shadows touching the red curve of her sensual mouth.

He settled more comfortably on the bar stool, took a look around. Down the bar, Mig waved. The juke box all but drowned the tinkle of ice and the clink of bottles. In a booth, a woman giggled shrilly. A drunk staggered toward the rest room. Hank came over. He wiped his damp rag over the bar.

"What'll it be, Mike?"

"Whiskey, Hank. Just ice." Mike glanced at Carla. "Buy you a drink?"

"For old time's sake?"

"Sure, Carla. For old time's sake."

He gave her a cigarette. Hank brought the drinks. She toasted him.

"To us."

"Why kid each other, Carla?"

"I'm not kidding." She paused. "I haven't seen much of you."

"I didn't figure you'd stay." Mike turned his head, blowing out a thin stream of smoke. When he looked back to her, he said, "According to what Ted tells me, you haven't been too lonely."

"What does that mean?"

"He said he stayed with you."

"Would you care?"

"No."

Carla smiled. She looked right at Mike.

"Mike," she said softly, "I think you're lying. All men care. I know. Even if you didn't want me, you wouldn't want anybody else to have me." She turned her head. "I know too much," she whispered. She stopped and then looked at Mike again. "But don't worry."

"Worry? What do you mean?"

"About Ted." She shrugged. "He's not going to bother me or any other woman."

"Why?"

"His wife."

"Go on, Carla."

"Oh, hell," she said suddenly. "I was nice to him only because I wanted to talk about you—but he's a creep. All hands. He got mean one night. I was afraid he'd kill me. Anyway, it didn't come to anything. In the end he was just a sick kid crying. Whatever he might have been, she ruined his confidence. He told me every time he tried to make love to her, she made him feel he'd failed. She laughed at him. Sure, he drinks and talks big but she's got him to where he has an inferiority complex a mile wide. One of these days, because he won't be able to stand thinking he's no good, he'll go out of his mind. For all I know, he'll end up killing somebody."

"It can't be that bad."

"Can't it?"

Carla sipped her drink.

"Mike," she said, "I don't want to talk about Ted. I don't want to talk about anything to do with men. Say something nice. Tell me a story. Tell me a joke. Make me laugh, Mike." She took a deep breath. "Oh, God, everything gets so mixed up."

"Yeah," Mike said. Was Carla trying to let him know that she was like other people? That she could suffer?

He signaled Hank for another pair of drinks. Out of the corner of his eye, he saw Mig watching him. Instead of black Capri pants she was wearing green ones, and a matching sweater. Her ridiculous orange hair was brushed up in a coil. Over the noise and the throbbing music, a gang in one of the booths yelled for service. Mig slipped through the crowd. At the bar, Hank served the drinks. The cash register clanged.

"Oh," Carla whispered. "For God's sakes."

Mike turned.

"What's wrong?"

"Look," She nodded toward the door. Ted and Holly were coming in.

Holly caught sight of them and waved.

Mike waved back.

She started toward the bar, but Ted caught her arm, thrust her behind him. His fists clenched, he advanced on Mike and Carla.

Here we go again, thought Mike. I hope I don't have to hit him …

CHAPTER SIX

MIKE WAS never sure just what woke him. A noise, a cry, a splash. Whatever it was, it startled all the sleep out of him. He sat straight up in his bunk, listening. Not a sound out of place, just the gentle lapping of the water at the float.

He looked at the clock. Four-fifteen. Too early in the morning for boats to want service. But he was sure he had heard something. He pulled on his khaki pants and hurried out of the shack.

He stood for a moment on the float, looking around, his eyes adjusting to the dark. And then he saw something—thought he saw something—a white speck in the water, almost at the shore, catching the light for a moment…

He sprinted toward land. There were still a few lights at the Blue Gull; probably Hank was cleaning up. Mike swung along the shore, breathing hard as he ran, his mind telling him he was being foolish, that he could have seen nothing but a sea gull.

Then he reached the place. Not imagined, and not a gull. It was a man, half floating, face down in the shallow wash in back of the old sardine cannery.

You don't float that way unless you're dead, Mike thought.

He waded out, dragged the body back to shore. He took a quick look. Stray light from the Blue Gull showed him Ted. The boy's thin face looking strangely peaceful, his hair wet and plastered to his skull.

The eyes were closed. Mike pulled up one eyelid and let it fall. The body still held a faint warmth. And Mike thought he could detect the trace of a pulse.

A moment later, working quickly and automatically, and sticking to old-style respiration on the hunch that it would get rid of water, Mike was straddling the body and giving it artificial respiration. He worked frantically for a few minutes, and then was rewarded by an attempt at a breath. He let out a couple of yells, trying to attract help. Nobody answered. Probably nobody heard, not even Hank. Christ, if someone would only come along to give him a hand. If he could stop for a minute. There was a machine at the Blue Gull, with oxygen.

Ted was alive, but he wasn't breathing, not by himself. So Mike kept working. As long as his big hands worked, there was air, getting into Ted's lungs, and water coming out. Finally, the brine stopped trickling. Shallow, rasping breathing began. Mike stood up and waited a spell, catching his own breath. He was bathed in sweat. He decided to risk leaving Ted.

Mike ran for the Blue Gull. As he had thought, Hank was still there, cleaning up, the door locked. The bartender pointed to the clock and shook his head as Mike pounded on the door.

"For God's sake, Hank, let me in," Mike shouted. "A man needs help."

Hank threw open the door.

"Call a doctor, an ambulance," Mike gasped. "It's Ted Adam—half drowned. In back of the old cannery."

Hank reached for the phone, calmly, as though this happened every day. He spoke a few words, then turned back to Mike.

"What happened? Will he live?"

Mike told what he knew in a couple of sentences. "I've got to get back and see if he's still breathing."

Hank pushed over half a tumbler of rye. "Swallow this —on the house. Doc will be along in a minute."

He rummaged behind the counter and came up with a long flashlight. “Signal with this. Doc will see you.”

Mike gulped the drink. It burned his throat, belted his blood. He grabbed the flashlight and ran.

Ted was still breathing when Mike got back; irregularly, barely perceptibly, but his chest was moving, all right.

Ted had never been much of a figure of a man. Now, under the bright glare of the flashlight, his thin clothes plastered by the water to his skinny frame, he looked pathetically frail. There was a trail of blood on him now, a thin seep from the back of his skull.

Doctor Bowman arrived, gruff and sleepy but efficient. He listened for a second, said, “Just about alive. Heart’s going, but fluttering.” His fingers felt the place on Ted’s head that was bleeding. “Probably fracture, certainly a concussion. Ambulance should be along any minute. Best not to move him without a stretcher.”

“I’d better tell old Jake,” Mike said.

“Leave the light here,” the doctor said. “Can you find your way without it?”

“Sure,” Mike said, pleased that the responsibility for Ted was no longer his. He started for the dock, and realized that while he had said old Jake, he had been thinking of Holly. Hell, this was no time to mix with her. It would be up to old Jake to tell her.

Yet Holly was the one who woke when Mike knocked on the door of the house. She came to let him in, a robe clutched over her. “Mike—what’s the matter? Has something happened?”

“It’s Ted,” Mike said, and explained. Holly opened her mouth and put her hand over it. Was there a brief, secret look of pleasure on her face, quickly masked? Or was he seeing things, because of what he knew, what he wanted?

They told old Jake, but the news bewildered him. He could not quite grasp what had happened. Mike was a little surprised to see the gentle efficiency with which Holly took him in hand. By the time she got him dressed and down to the road, the ambulance was there and Ted was being carried up the slope, Doc Bowman giving orders.

The stretcher was slipped into the ambulance; old Jake and Holly prepared to follow. All of a sudden, Mike felt superfluous. A few people had gathered now, late drivers stopped by the ambulance lights and their curiosity. Mike felt like one of them, an outsider, watching like any morbid sightseer. But Holly turned to him before getting in. "Aren't you coming, Mike?"

"Don't think so," Mike said. "Somebody has to mind the store."

Old Jake nodded approvingly, and Holly climbed in with a flare of skirts and a flash of bare legs.

Next morning, a few minutes after Mike had finished sluicing the floats, the fat, swarthy deputy sheriff from the Slat Landing substation came down to the fuel dock. His name was Monty Gomez. His badge glittered in the hot sunshine.

"Hi, Mike."

Mike flipped off the burner under the coffee pot and walked outside to where Monty stood on the float. The wash of a passing boat made a soft lapping sound. The low mutter of diesel exhaust drifted across the water. Mike fumbled for a cigarette.

"What's up, Monty?"

"This is business, Mike."

"Business?" Mike frowned. "Oh. How's Ted?"

"Still alive," Monty said. "What happened?"

Mike gave him the story.

Monty nodded. "You were at the Blue Gull last night?"

"Sure."

"You had an argument with Ted Adam?"

Mike grinned.

"Hell," he said. "It wasn't much of an argument. There were a few words. I said hello to his wife. Ted told me not to talk to her. He took a swing at me. My God, Monty, you know Ted. I didn't want to clip him, so I left. Ted was drunk. He'd been drinking all day." Mike blew smoke in a thin stream. "Well, that's all there was to it. I came down here and turned in. I figured Ted could get home under his own power. It wasn't any of my business, as long as that was the way he felt."

"Yeah. I figured. But I've got a few questions."

"Like what?" Mike said. He had known Monty a long time.

"This is routine, Mike. Right now, it's just routine. Ted has a bad concussion, possibly a blood clot on the brain. He's in a coma—maybe he'll live, maybe not. He could have hurt his head falling. Or somebody could have slugged him and then thrown him into the water to drown. We know you had an argument. Didn't you tell Ted to be careful and not to start anything he couldn't finish?"

"Sure," Mike said. "But Monty—for God's sakes, I wouldn't lay for Ted."

"Did you?"

"No."

"He was drunk. It would have been easy."

"I wouldn't have done it. He must have stumbled. Staggered over the edge, somewhere."

"I hope you're right," Monty said. "But you had an argument with him earlier—and so far, you're the only person who heard him in the water, if that's what you did hear."

"Then why would I save him?" Mike asked. "If I'd done that to him, I would have let him die, wouldn't I? Why would I break my neck trying to save him? And I've known Ted all his life... Why would I do a thing like that to him?"

Monty shrugged. "I just mentioned it," he said. "You might have changed your mind after you saw what you'd done. You might have figured he would die anyway, and you wouldn't be suspected this way. And Ted never had a wife before, when you were around. I just hope you're in the clear, because there's going to be talk. And if Ted dies, as he might well do, there would be a coroner's inquest. Right now, it's an accident or assault—but it could develop into murder."

All through the rest of the day, gradually fitting the pieces together, Mike could not forget the way Monty had looked at him. The old man was hard to take, too. Like someone who had been hit by a club, old Jake had a stunned expression in his watery eyes. They had come back from the hospital with no news. Ted was in a coma. They would not be allowed to see him for a while, probably several days at least. The hospital would call if there were any change.

Sitting in the kitchen, drinking hot, black coffee, talking to Mike, to Holly, to Gomez and the sheriff, to neighbors and old school friends of Ted's, old Jake would lose track of what had happened and begin to look around and ask where Ted had gone.

"He's a good boy," he whispered. "You've known him a long time, Mike. Isn't he a good boy?"

"Sure," Mike lied.

"After his mother died, he was all I had. Of course, now I got Holly, too."

"Don't worry, Pa." Holly refilled the coffee cups. Then, slipping her arm around Jake's shoulders, she kissed his weathered cheek. "He'll be all right."

"Yes, he'll be all right," the old man said, as though he did not believe it at all. "I'm luckier'n some, though, 'cause now I got Holly."

After some of the people had gone, old Jake asked about the argument Mike and Ted had gotten into. "They said you two almost come to fighting."

"It wasn't anything, Jake."

"You're sure?"

"He had a few drinks too many," Mike said. He turned and looked at Holly. With her blond hair brushed back, her plain blue cotton house dress simple, buttoned high at her throat, she did not look even nineteen. For one thing, she wore almost no make-up. Besides, she had somehow subdued the natural vitality that usually made her eyes so alive. To all appearances, she was just the quiet, numbed, suffering wife. Without tears, she gave the impression of deep sadness. To Jake, she was all loving tenderness. Never once, in the smallest way, did she give a hint to Mike that she was not grieving for Ted. Her restrained manner caused the people who visited to call her brave. But Mike remembered naked slenderness, hair loose and skin smooth as silk, lips clinging, begging, body shuddering.

"Mike," Jake piped, "you say Ted had a few drinks?" "That's right, Jake."

"The sheriff said there was another woman over there at the Blue Gull."

"That's right, Jake. A woman named Carla. She's an old friend of mine."

Oh, sure. That Hollywood one. Ted knew her?"

"A little."

"Well," Jake said. "He's a good boy. He's not the kind to fool with another woman. That's right, isn't it, Holly?"

"Yes, Pa."

Ted loves you. He's a good boy," the old man said. "I sent him money to go to college. He studied hard. Maybe too hard. He never drank too much until then but he wanted me to be proud of him. I'm sorry you and him argued, Mike."

"It wasn't anything."

"Why, you two were friends in school. God damn it," the old man sniffled. He blinked, rubbing his knuckles across his eyes. "I worked all my life to give good things to my boy." He looked up suddenly. "By the way, Holly, where is Ted now?"

"Pa, Ted's in the hospital."

Oh—that's right. Sure. A man my age gets mixed up now and then." He paused, fumbling, clumsily filling his pipe. With shaking hand he struck a match. It burned smokily. The flame sucked down. He puffed. "Don't seem like there is any justice in this world. I worked hard. I tried to do right. I just don't understand why this had to happen."

"Don't, Pa," Holly whispered. She sat down, patting his hand. Tears sparkled in her eyes. Softly, hopelessly, she talked about how she had tried to get Ted to come home with her from the Blue Gull. "But he was stubborn, Pa."

"You couldn't help what happened, Holly."

"Maybe. I guess I should have stayed with him—but you know how he runs off by himself. When I came home and went to bed I thought he's just taken the car and gone back over to Monterey. Then when I woke up—" She stopped, bowing her head. "Pa, how will I ever forgive myself?"

"It wasn't your fault."

Holly wiped her eyes. For a little while longer, she went on, talking about how Ted must have stumbled coming down half asleep. Then, after closing the old man's bedroom door, she returned to the kitchen.

"Holly, it's been a hard day. Guess I'd better go on down to the shack."

She lifted her face. "Mike?"

"Yes?"

"Aren't you going to kiss me?"

She extended a hand. The tips of her fingers touched his mouth. She moved, turning against him. Her arms went around his neck. She parted her lips, hugging tightly as he bent to kiss her mouth. The tip of her tongue traced fire but suddenly, shivering, she twisted away from him.

"Not now, Mike."

"I love you."

"Yes," she whispered. "I know, Mike. But we've got to wait. We've got to be careful." Her voice trembled. "The doctor told me Ted had little chance to live. If he dies, I'll eventually get old Jake's money. Oh, God, Mike," she finished breathlessly, "I want to be rich."

CHAPTER SEVEN

THE NEXT day, Mike saw Holly for only a few minutes — in the morning when she was hanging out some washing. Albacore were running less than a hundred miles off shore and Mike had a steady succession of tuna trollers to fuel. Late in the afternoon most of the boats had left the harbor but by that time Holly had gone off with old Jake to visit Ted. Before they got back for supper, Monty Gomez came down to the dock.

By then, a low night fog had drifted in from the sea. The lights of the shack blurred mistily and for a few moments, smoking a cigarette with Mike, Monty chatted about the weather. It was summer. Fog was to be expected. They were lucky to have had some real hot summer for a change. Of course, the fishermen weren't going to like the poor visibility. Monty paused, listening to the fog horn on the point. Before he could go on, Mike interrupted him, said they might as well get to the point.

"What are you after, Monty?"

"Just visiting, Mike."

"What about Ted? Did you decide it was an accident?"

"It looks that way."

"What's that suppose to mean?"

"Nothing special, Mike. You and Holly and this Carla woman were all more or less involved in that little debate with Ted. As a matter of fact, Mig had a little argument too. She took your side after you left the Blue Gull."

"My God, you don't think Mig pushed Ted into the slough."

"No," Monty said slowly. "I just said it looks like it was an accident. Of course, Ted knew that path. Seems funny he'd fall over the side after all the years he's lived around here. Anyway, we're just checking around. I don't guess you've got any worries."

"You don't guess. Is that a threat?"

"Why would I threaten you, Mike?"

"That's what I want to know."

"No reason, is there?"

"No," Mike said. "None."

"Then," Monty said easily, "don't mind me." He remarked, then, that he had talked to Carla and Mig and Holly and the old man; he remarked that Ted's accident had been a shock to all of them. Then he asked some questions about the fighting Mike had done in the ring and, along with that, he casually mentioned he had heard Mike might be interviewed by some people in San Francisco interested in taking the lid off crooked fights. "I guess," Monty finished, "You saw some pretty dirty things."

"A few, maybe."

Mike let it go at that and, a little later Monty took his leave.

God damn him—Mike knew the deputy was not satisfied. He was sure as hell going to keep on snooping. Let him, then. Mike had not shoved Ted into the slough. Holly hadn't, either. She had been at home and in her bed. That was her story. Story? Mike swore softly. He was innocent. Holly was innocent. That was that. To hell with suspicion. That was Monty's job. Anyway, anything could happen to a drunk. Ted had fallen. It was an accident. Nobody could make anything else out of it. Why should they? But an hour or so later, when he changed into fresh clothes and went up to the house, he found Holly and the old man thinking about Monty, too.

"I told him, Mike," Jake said. "I told Monty that Ted didn't have enemies. Everybody liked Ted. Ain't that right, Holly?"

"Yes, Pa."

"Ted's a good boy. Hell, Mike went to school with Ted. Ain't that right, Mike?"

"Yes," Mike said. "That's right."

"You two were always friends. What's the matter with that Monty?"

Jake nodded to himself. Then, after insisting Mike have something to eat, the old man spent the meal muttering, remembering, talking about what a good boy Ted had always been. Later, while Holly did the dishes, Jake got drowsy and, finally, taking one of the sleeping pills the doctor had left, shuffled off to his bed.

For a while longer, Mike and Holly stayed in the kitchen. She mixed drinks and then, going to her bedroom, she called to Mike to come help with her dress. "Unzip me, Mike."

"Hey, not so loud!"

"Don't worry, Jake won't wake up now."

"Holly."

"Yes?"

"This is Ted's room."

"Don't talk about him, Mike. Talk about us."

She turned, standing with her back to him. The small light on the bedside table reflected in the mirror. On the dresser top, a perfume bottle glittered. Golden tints shimmered in her honey-blond hair. Outside, a truck rattled past the house. The sound of the fog horn came softly. Mike breathed deeply and then, moving his hand, he slid down the zipper. As her dress parted, her bare shoulders and the tawny sleekness of her slim back caught warm creamy shadows. She wriggled. The dress slipped over her flaring hips and fell to the floor. Nylon glistened. She lifted her arms, unhooking her bra. A moment later, stepping out of her panties, she turned nakedly, looking up, whispering his name.

"Mike?"

"Yes."

"Am I beautiful?"

"Yes, Holly."

"Turn out the lights, Mike."

"Are you sure?"

"Yes, Mike," she whispered. "I know what I want."

Her lips waited for him, the hot curve of her mouth yielding and then, on the bed, turning her cheek against the pillow, she surrendered, huddling hungrily in the closeness of his arms.

"Mike," she begged.

"Yes."

"I love you."

She moved, crying softly, shuddering. Her arms went around his neck.

"Mike," she moaned. "Oh, God, Mike."

His lips on her breasts. His hands full of golden flesh. Her fingers at his back, fondling; at his thighs, seeking. Satin skin. Red mouth.

They shifted, stretched side by side, mouth on red mouth and loin to groin. "Oh, don't torture me," she gasped. "Don't torture me any more." And she rolled on top of him, he moving to his back, and in unabashed eagerness she used him. He panted and clutched her. It was that rocket to the moon again, that detonation like a bursting galaxy.

They shook in the teeth of bliss, in the agonized culmination; flesh on flesh, around flesh, in flesh. And she deserted the seat of love as exhausted as he. But not for long. They sprawled, recovering breath, and suddenly she was up.

He felt the liquid fire, the teasing tongue. He felt the caress of her perfumed hair.

Anything.

She had meant it.

In his unendurable pleasure, sharp as knives, he groaned. "Holly, Holly!"

A long time later, he moved away from her. Sliding to the edge of the bed, he found his shirt. His fingers trembled.

"Cigarette, Holly?"

"Yes, Mike."

She stretched, darkness curving the lift of her breasts. The looseness of her hair tangled over her bare shoulder. In the flickering glow of his lighter, shadows flattened across her stomach. Dampness glistened the satin sheen of her slim figure. Flame reflected in her eyes as he lit the cigarettes.

"Thanks, Mike."

He turned, looking down at her.

"Holly."

"Yes."

"You said you loved me."

"I do, Mike."

He waited. Tobacco smoke twisted up into the darkness. The red tip of her cigarette glowed. He saw her darkly. Traffic hummed and bumbled along the highway. On the road outside the window, some kids laughed. Footsteps pattered, but Mike kept looking at Holly.

Anything.

Just ask me.

The beat of the words hammered out the truth in his brain. He remembered the lifting, the taut clinging, the melting heat, the thrusting, the whirlpooling into glittering ecstasy. It would always be that way with her. Perfect. He remembered the bursting bliss, the oneness, the instant when he had had everything. It had never been that way with Carla. It had never been that way with any other woman.

"Holly," he whispered. "I want you to marry me."

"No. Not now, Mike."

"All right," he said slowly. "I know you'll have to wait until Ted is out of the hospital or dies. But there's no reason we should pretend. Let's make up our minds and then let's tell everybody. The hell with this sneaking, this doing things behind Ted's back—behind Jake's back."

Holly sat up.

"No," she said.

"Why?"

She reached for the ash tray. When he handed it to her, she squashed out her cigarette.

"Holly," Mike said. "You didn't answer. Why should we hide?"

She frowned. "Mike," she said patiently. "We've got to wait."

"Because of old Jake's money?"

"Yes."

"You said that you love me."

"I do."

"Isn't that enough?"

"No." Holly moved, curling around to Mike. "Listen," she whispered. "This is my chance. I have to wait. I'm so near it."

"Jake's money?"

"Yes."

"Money isn't worth it, Holly."

"It is to me." She paused and then, suddenly, bitterly, her voice edged with hardness, she started telling how she had grown up. "Nothing," she whispered. "All my life, I had nothing. Maybe that's all right for a boy but it's hell for a girl. My folks came up here to work in the fields around Salinas. Stoop labor, thinning lettuce and field vegetables. All my life was spent in dirty little dumps. Shanty life. Don't tell me I don't need money. I never even had a decent pair of shoes. We came up here from East Texas, river country. My father existed by swampland grubbing. He couldn't even read or write. He didn't give a damn, either. He didn't need learning —he didn't want any. He was satisfied and he expected me to be satisfied. When I was going to high school and needed some nice clothes, he told me to go out and peddle a little. He meant it. So far as he was concerned, I was just a mouth that cost money to feed. Well, let me tell you something. I didn't intend to end up following crops with a bunch of snot-nosed kids pawing at me. By the time I was fifteen I knew I didn't have to do that. God knows, I soon found out what I had. Mike, experts tried to rape me ... But I'm not crying. In this world you get what you've got the nerve to take. Nobody wants tears and I'm not going to waste my time lying either. When I met Ted, I knew he was going to end up getting his father's money. So I got Ted to marry me."

"Holly," Mike whispered. "Listen—"

"No," she said furiously. "You listen. I've already earned my share. I've gone through hell with Ted. He has a mind like a gutter. He doesn't know how to love or to be loved. He just knows how to hurt, to get everything in his dirty hands. He hates me because I knew he was no good but that never stopped him from being a sneaky little liar. He lies to everybody. Even his father. There wasn't any college. Ted started but that was as far as he got. Only he never gave up milking the old man for the allowance he got to go to school. But Ted never went near a school. Up in San Francisco, we lived in a dirty little hotel. As long as Ted didn't have to work, he was satisfied. Oh, God," Holly finished miserably. "Don't tell me it's wrong to want old Jake's money. And even if it were, it wouldn't matter. Everything in this world is wrong, anyway. Every day, people cheat and lie. Winning is all that counts. Nobody likes a loser. Well, Mike. I don't intend to lose. I intend to win."

"How about me?"

"We can wait, Mike."

"How long?"

"I don't know, Mike." She took a deep breath. "We'll wait as long as we have to wait."

"What does that mean?"

"Mike," she said softly, "Ted is still in a coma. They tell me it's more than likely he'll never come out of it. After that, there's only the old man—and nobody lives forever."

CHAPTER EIGHT

FOR A LONG time that night, Mike lay awake in the shack. Fog misted the dark windows. Harbor sounds drifted across the still water. The fuel dock float creaked, surging to the ebbing tide. Somewhere ashore, a dog barked. Above, on the road, cars passed, headlights gleamed.

Anything.

Just ask me.

Mike went over it in his mind. The naked sleekness came back, the curving warmth of Holly lifting, begging, the hot hunger of her mouth. His hands still felt the slender satin smoothness, the crush of her breasts. She knew how to give, how to belong until she was completely possessed. He breathed in memory the flowery breath of her, the sweet woman fragrance. He saw the damp flare of her hair loose against the pillow. He thought of the taut bow, of the pleading; he heard those last lingering whispers, the quick intake of her breathing. He left the trembling passion of her yielding, surrendering.

Did these add up to love?

The question circled in his head as sleep gathered, brought him as in a remembered dream back to beginnings. Restlessly, he knew smallness again, the cannery smell of Slat Landing, the raw bare ugliness, the windswept sand, scrunty grass, junk, rotting old boats, the dust and stink of the chemical plant, the wire-fenced gray hulk of the power plant, the dead barren evaporation beds where drying salt turned bloody red with a kind of brine shrimp. Once more, dirty in ragged blue jeans and frayed canvas shoes, he was watching the big sardine purse-seiners come in loaded, their decks awash. Year after year, taking everything, accusing anybody who got in their way of being stupid, the fishermen and canneries gutted the sea, netting hundreds of thousands of tons of fish. When there were too many to can, fertilizer was made out of them. The landing reeked with the stinking greediness and then the fish were no more.

Mike had been ten or eleven when the canneries had begun closing. As if meeting himself in a mirror, in a dream, Mike was there again, romping with the other kids past the empty loading ramps. He heard fishermen say wind or ocean currents had shifted, would shift back; the fish would show up again. Nobody ever admitted the sardines had been fished out, killed, netted, until Slat Landing was rotting buildings and crumbling machinery.

Drunks slept under the foundations. Mike's father was one of them. Sometimes, if he worked, they rented a room. Half the time there would be some fat old slut slopping around. Working at odd jobs, finding places to hide out along the mud flats, salvaging junk from the litters of broken bottles and rusting tin cans, Mike raised himself.

Toward the end, when Mike was of high-school age, the old man got so crippled that he could hardly move; but he could still drink. In the shed Mike made grocery money by helping out on weekends in the boat yards. The old man would steal it to buy whiskey or wine.

Now, in his bunk, Mike dreamed his father's voice, the way he had looked that last cold winter night when he had died. It had been raining that week. The shed had been damp, musty with the smell of dirty bedclothes. The old man hadn't shaved. On the floor beside his bed he had dropped an empty wine bottle but when he had awakened, calling to Mike that last time, the old man had been cold sober.

"Mike," he had croaked. "Come here."

Mike had lit a lamp, and had gone to him. Sweat had been glittering on his father's forehead. The old man had moved feverishly, wetting his dry lips with the tip of his tongue.

"Mike."

"Yes, Pa. There's no wine left. No whiskey, nothing."

"I know." The old man had held on to Mike with shaking hands. He had talked about the years when Mike's mother had been alive. After that he had closed his eyes for a while.

"Pa," Mike said, "I better get a doctor."

"No, boy. Too late. Just let me rest."

That had been the end.

After that, Mike knocked around on his own, fighting, building a little local reputation before going into the Marines. He went on boxing in the service. When he got out, he worked the big live-bait tuna clippers going south and then he met Fat Joe.

Money, after that. Money to spend.

And Carla.

He had really had the world by the tail. Big shot, Mike Shannon. Just sign here. Don't read any contracts. Let Fat Joe do the thinking. The blur spiraled—glamor, bright lights; the sweat and the smell of leather, too. He'd had it all and those gut-tightening moments up the ladder to the ring, the ropes, the quick movements of his feet, loosening up, biting down on the mouth piece and the announcer pointing.

"In this corner, Mike Shannon—"

Mike could whip anybody.

He had really believed it. Why not? Fat Joe, Carla, the trainers, the sparring partners, the whole parade patted his back. And nights with Carla, he got what he wanted and believed it was love.

Love...

The word exploded. Mike woke in his bunk. He didn't want that love again, in or out of a dream. He didn't want to fight that last fight again, either. He hated the helplessness, when all he had was courage. Afterward the papers had called him a toy tiger but the gamblers had made their killing. It was over. Get out. Tell him, Carla. Kiss that chump off. Mike smoked a cigarette before trying to go back to sleep. Money. Yeah, it had been nice while it lasted. Maybe Holly was right. A hundred thousand. Just to say it sounded good. He closed his eyes, rolled over.

Money.

A hundred thousand.

The look in Holly's eyes came back.

After that, there's only the old man—and nobody lives forever…

Late the next morning when Mig came down to the fuel dock to say hello to him, Mike got a look at the other side of the coin.

By then the fog had cleared. Sunlight glittered on the water. The sky was a California blue and Mig looked fresh and slender in a white dress and white sandals. Her hair was no longer orange but had been dyed—of all things—a delicate pink. Wind fluttered her skirt and when Mike finished pumping fuel into a rebuilt wartime barge that a grubby crew used for fishing crabs, she crossed to the shack, waiting while Mike wrote out the bill.

"Mig," Mike said then, "you shouldn't come down here."

"And why shouldn't I?"

"Didn't you see that crew giving you the eye?"

"Well?"

"They give you the eye because you give them ideas." "How about you?"

"I've always had those ideas."

"But this is so sudden! You never told me, Mike."

"No," he said. "I didn't. I always figured you were too good for me."

"That's a funny thing to say."

"It's true."

Mig shook her head.

"No," she said softly. "I'm not good, Mike. I never was good. Not the way you mean." She turned her head and the slant of sunlight shadowed her breasts. Pinkness blazed from the silkiness of her hair. In the channel a tug passed. Water frothed away from the tug's bow, spreading wavelets. On the far shore, two little girls in short skirts waded out into the weedy shallows and then Mig whispered, "Nobody knows much about anybody else, Mike. When you were fighting, I used to think I'd never see you again. I hated seeing your picture in the papers, thinking you were too famous to remember me. Envy is funny, isn't it? I wanted you to fail. If you got beaten, I figured, you would come home. Yet all that time, Mike, I was married. You never met Herb, did you? Well, you will. He comes over to watch me. Only now I'm free. He can't get mean and slap me around. Yes," she said bitterly. "I've been beaten too. Only it's different for a woman. I knew he was getting something out of it, something sick and ugly. It used to get crazy in his eyes when he watched me crawl up. I hated him for it but it wasn't all one-sided, Mike. I think I wanted to be punished and hurt. I never loved him. I got married the way kids do. He was there. All my friends were married. I didn't want to carry a torch the rest of my life. You didn't know that. Well it's true."

"You don't have to tell me things, Mig, you don't have to bare yourself."

"I want to." She looked up. "On my wedding night, that first time, holding me, Herb wanted me to tell him I loved him. I told him but I lied. I think he always knew that. Maybe I made him what he ended up being." She shrugged. "Anyway, it's over. You're back." Her smile trembled. "And you see, Mike? I'm not really good at all."

"Yes, Mig. You're so good that you're odd. Like your hair. Pink is nicer than orange, though."

She laughed. "Oh, that's to show people I'm independent. That I'm me. You understand, don't you?" She changed the subject, asking a few questions about Carla. Mike answered without really saying anything and finally Mig told him that her excuse for visiting was old Jake. She had been up to the house to see if Holly needed any help. "I knew Ted's accident must have hit them both pretty hard."

"It did, Mig. Especially Jake."

"I know. I talked to Ted just before he left the Blue Gull. He was mumbling about seeing that Carla woman but I guess he never got to the hotel. Anyway, that's what I told Monty."

"So he's been questioning you too?"

"Yes," Mig said. "I don't mind. Besides, that was the last I saw of Ted so I don't have much to tell." She paused. "I just hope Monty didn't upset Holly. She's been wonderful through all of this. I'll admit I never really liked her before. I guess a lot of us were guilty of that, but I'm not afraid to admit I was wrong. She's being so good to old Jake."

"Like a real daughter, Mig."

"I think they're both lonely. She's young and he's old but right now they need each other."

Mike nodded. "I guess so."

"Well, Mike, I can tell you this much. Jake just adores her. His eyes shone with tears when I was up to the house. He blesses her name and she deserves it. Most girls her age wouldn't bother their heads about him. He's just lucky."

Lucky?

A hundred thousand. All the property.

No other relatives. Just Ted and Holly.

"Sure," Mike said. "Jake is lucky."

"So long," Mig said. "See you around. And I'll try not to be envious any more."

"Envious of what?"

"Of the girl who gets you," Mig said.

She tossed her pink hair. He caught a good view of her legs as she climbed the steps.

CHAPTER NINE

ON the following Saturday, Carla telephoned.

"Mike, I've got to see you. Come over to the hotel." Mike remarked that he had heard she had left Slat Landing. "Only for a few days, Mike. I made a little trip to Los Angeles."

"To talk to Fat Joe?"

"I didn't say that."

"No," Mike replied. "But it figures. You and Fat Joe must have seen the release in Monday's paper. It seems that two fighters and three managers have already been interviewed. I'm next on the list. They're going to talk to Goofy, too. Remember Goofy, my trainer?"

"What if I told you that you were wrong?"

"You'd be lying."

"Mike, don't you have any faith?"

"No," he said. "Not any more."

"Well," Carla said slowly. She stopped. A moment passed. "Oh," she said finally, "all right. I did see Fat Joe."

"It's nice to know I was right."

"Please, Mike. Why do you want to plant needles?" Her voice broke. "Can't you be nice? I tell you that you've got to come over."

"Suppose I don't?"

"I'd have to make trouble, Mike."

"For me?"

"Yes."

"You can't hurt me any more, Carla."

"Yes," she said. "I can."

"How?"

"Mike, I could say that I saw you push Ted Adam into the water?"

"You bitch," he growled.

"All right, call me names. But come. Say eight o'clock?" "I don't have much choice."

"No," Carla said softly. "You don't."

Working through the afternoon, Mike had plenty of time to think about what Carla had said. But toward evening Jake came down to help run the dock. Mike did not let on that anything was wrong. He chatted a while, and listened to the old man's troubles.

"I have a hard time sleeping. But those pills help." "Don't take too many."

"Oh," Jake said. "I don't have to worry. Holly watches out for me. It's pretty lonely without Ted."

"I guess you're right."

"But I got Holly. I'm a lucky man. Come on up and eat with us."

"Sure," Mike said. "Then I won't be lonely, either." Upstairs, Mike met Holly on the back porch.

"All dressed up, Mike?"

"Well," he said. "These gray slacks are the best I've got."

"You look nice."

"Thanks."

"Is that all?"

Mike breathed the sweet fragrance of her. Darkness shadowed the soft cleavage of her breasts. The skirt of her yellow cotton dress fluttered against her bare legs. A loose wisp of blond hair blew silkily against her cheek. After glancing down at the fuel dock where the old man was puttering at the pumps, Mike looked into Holly's eyes.

"What else is there to say?"

"Does that mean you're angry?"

"No," Mike said. "It means I'm not seeing much of you these days."

"Jake needs me."

"I don't need you?"

"Mike," she said softly, "don't spoil things. This is for you, too."

"Me?"

"Yes," she said. "I want us to have everything." "Including Jake's money?"

"Yes. Is that so awful?"

Mike waited. The old man had got a hammer and was pounding a nail into the railing at the back of the shack. The sound reverberated across the water. At the head of the slough the auxiliary refrigerating engine of a salmon boat chugged. Two kids were rowing an old skiff toward the swampy tide flats. The splash of the oars and the voices drifted across the water. In an insane kind of way, Mike was aware of everything and at the same time aware only of the warm closeness of Holly, the dark curve of her mouth, her eyes looking up into his, Mike counted the way he wanted her, calculated against the way she was cuddling Jake. What the hell was right? Was there any solid answer or was each thing right or wrong according to who did it? My God, the world had plenty of people waiting for other people to die. Why not Holly?

"Well," she said. "You didn't answer me, Mike. Is it so awful to want Jake's money?"

"Holly, I don't know."

"Somebody will get it, eventually."

"Nobody takes it with him," he agreed.

"Mike," she whispered. "I want it for us."

"It might not be that easy."

Holly turned her head and looked down at the fuel dock. The old man moved in the glare of the shack lights. "He ought to be careful," she said. "Those railings are rotten. If one broke, he could easily fall into the water. You'd think, working around boats, Pa would have learned to swim. Ted's the same way. He can't swim, either."

"Oh?"

She studied Mike's face.

"Didn't you know?"

"No."

"Well, it's true." She stopped. "It's just one of those thing you're bound to think about."

"Maybe."

"Don't be angry, Mike."

"I'm not angry."

"Well then," she said. "Just because I say what is true, don't hate me."

"Holly," Mike said slowly, "I couldn't hate you."

"Ever? You're sure?"

"I could never hate you."

"I'm glad," Holly whispered. "I want you to have me. I've got so much to give. Oh, God, Mike every night, even though we can't be together, I go over everything, I live everything again. I do it all with you." Her lips trembled. "I want to belong to you forever, Mike. I want us to be married, want it as much as you do. Oh, I hope we don't have to wait too long..."

"Don't say it that way, Holly."

"How else can I say it?"

They watched Jake come puffing to get his pipe. He stayed on, dirty, grunting, sniffling, chewing his gums, hugging his arm over Holly's shoulder and saying he didn't see how he could ever get along without her.

"Don't worry, Pa. I'll always take care of you. You have a home, and you have a daughter."

"Well," Jake said softly, "it's your house as much as mine." He blinked his eyes, squeezing Holly. "I'm lucky, Mike."

"What's the latest report on Ted?"

"Still unconscious. They feed him through his veins. But he'll pull through. Won't he pull through, Mike?"

Mike nodded, and left them together. He walked slowly in the darkness but he could not make heads or tails of the way he felt about Holly at the moment. Did he love her? Honest to God, he had seen plenty of womanly artifice in his day but she had it down to a fine art. I ought to hate her, Mike thought. He stared at the sagging outlines of the crumbling sardine cannery. It loomed like a huge faceless monster. A broken window pane caught a slant of light and glittered icily. Darkly, a bat swooped out of the shadows. Hate? Could hate emerge like a bat? Dirt and loose gravel crunched. Mike lit a cigarette. Tobacco burned in his throat. Holly, Holly! Her name circled the rim of his mind. The clutch of a fist raked his stomach. His loins recalled the golden darkness, a warmth twisting in his arms, the hot seeking of her mouth. Holly. He inhaled. The hot tip of his cigarette glowed red. A gust of wind blew cool sea mist. The dull boom of surf came from where the breakwater sheltered the entrance to the harbor. Holly! Please—my Holly! Oh, God, stop. He inhaled again. The neon glare of the Blue Gull flooded garish light across the rutted road. Mike turned toward the hotel and glanced at his watch. It was two minutes to eight.

He walked upstairs and rapped Carla's door. The latch clicked.

"Hello, Mike. Come in."

She stepped aside and in a swift appraisal he measured her against Holly. They were both on the small side, slender; but where Holly was fair, Carla was dark. Where Holly was fresh, Carla was polished, showing a sleek kind of expensiveness that gave her an exotic warmth. She had the smoothness of ripe fruit and even in the black bedroom negligee, the slender curves of her body blending into the long, shapely legs, she breathed a poised feminine confidence. Her dark hair was brushed back, coiled and alive with light. Lipstick defined the perfect curve of her mouth.

The filmy, silky fabric moved softly against the upward thrust of her firm breasts. She lifted her face and then, closing the door, she smiled.

"Seen enough?"

"Was I staring? I'm sorry."

"Don't be, Mike. I want you to look. Otherwise, this get-up would be wasted."

"You're a beautiful woman, Carla."

"Thank you." She paused, waiting, but Mike made no move to touch her. She shrugged. "I guess," she said, "that you've forgotten."

"Forgotten?"

"We used to be in love."

"Is that what you call it?"

"Mike," Carla whispered, "it was real. We were going to be married."

"Sure," Mike said. "I haven't forgotten, darling. That was one of Fat Joe's more involved gags. He always provided everything. Even women. Take no chances. Hire the best. You must have cost plenty, but I'll say this, Carla—you knew all the tricks. How did you and Joe work it out? Was it piecework? So much a lay?"

"Please, Mike. I've asked you not to talk like that."

"Why? Don't you like the truth? Hell, Carla, business is business."

He walked away from her and inspected the room. There was a hotel tray on the dresser. It held a fifth of whiskey, a mixer and a bowl of ice. The window drapes were drawn. By the bed, a blue-shaded lamp shed soft light. Everything was ready. The prostitute knew her trade. Now came the big pitch. Be nice, Mike. Keep your mouth shut. Don't cause any trouble for Fat Joe and Carla will be nice to you. Mike lit a cigarette but when he turned, facing her again, telling her what he thought, she shook her head.

"No, Mike," she whispered. "You've got it wrong."

"Wrong?" Mike held his cigarette between his thumb and forefinger. Smoke curled over his hand. Light reflected on the smooth planes of Carla's cheeks. A trace of moisture listened where she had touched the pink tip of her tongue to her lipstick. Outside the room, in the hall, footsteps passed. Somewhere in the building a door slammed and with the sound, his voice harsh, Mike went on, "I haven't got it wrong, Carla. I've got it right. As soon as it was mentioned I might talk to newspaper people about crooks like Fat Joe, he sent you up here. Before that, I could have dropped dead and he wouldn't have blinked an eye. Why should he? After all, he had used me up. You don't spend money or time on a dead horse or a fighter who has hit the road to nowhere. Do you think I'm still stupid? No, don't stop me. I've got eyes. Everything is ready. You haven't got a damn thing on under that gown. You gave it to me when you first got here, and now you're ready to give it to me again. Money won't buy me off, but fancy sex might. Well, baby, that suits me just fine. I know what you can do, so I'm not walking out of here. But I'm not kidding myself, either. It's all on the house but it isn't free. Fat Joe always has a price." Mike laughed. "Actually, I feel flattered. I didn't know I was so important." "All right, Mike."

"Aren't you going to argue?"

"No."

"Fat Joe did send you?"

"Yes."

"Why bother with me? No matter what I say to reporters, it would be just my word. He could deny everything." "He's going into politics, Mike. He doesn't want any bad publicity right now."

Mike said, "Suppose I feel like spilling everything I know, anyway?"

"I've already told you, Mike." Carla's voice trembled. Dampness sparkled in her dark lashes. "If you won't agree to be sensible, I'll go to the police and tell them I saw you push Ted

Adam off the path that night." "Carla," Mike said, "you couldn't make that stick."

"It wouldn't matter, Mike."

"How do you figure?"

"If you were suspected of a crime," Carla said, "your

word would carry no weight at all. The newspapers would be bound to make a lot out of a plot by you and Holly."

"Holly?"

"She's young and blond and beautiful."

"So?"

"Mike," Carla whispered. "You don't have to lie to me. A woman knows. There is love between you."

"I suppose you told Fat Joe that, too."

"Yes."

"You are rotten. You don't have even a whore's honor." "No, Mike. You don't understand."

Mike turned his back and walked to the dresser. Savagely he ground out his cigarette. Then he opened the fifth. Whiskey gurgled, splashing into the glass. Christ, that Fat Joe missed no bets. Suppose Carla did spring the lie. There would be buckets of trouble no matter how it turned out eventually. Even if he managed to prove her story false, she could get off the hook by pleading mistaken identity. All Fat Joe needed was the threat. Mike lifted the glass. Whiskey flamed in his throat. Get on top and tramp the guy beneath you. That was Fat Joe's method and why pretend? It worked. He had the money, he had the power. Why buck it? Holly was bound to get involved and, if it ever came out that she had slept with Mike there would be all hell to pay. Anyway, who ever got any medals for being a big pure hero? Suppose he did spill what he knew? After a couple of days in the spotlight, he would be just another washed-out fighter again; as far as that went, when it was all over and the dust settled, the same gang would be doing the same kind of business at the same old stand.

"Mike. Look at me."

He turned. She was close. Through the filmy lace he could see her rich breasts curving, the dark nipples beckoning. Below the loosely tied belt, the slit of the robe released the golden nakedness of her thigh. Light shimmered in her dark hair. Her eyes were pools of urging, of invitation.

"Don't worry," he said. "I've thought it over. I've got the message and I'm not going to be any crusader. Tell Fat Joe. You keep your mouth shut and I'll keep my mouth shut. Great, isn't it?"

"Don't resent me. Don't spill your contempt on me, Mike."

"Why not?" He reached, hooking his fingers in the filmy folds. She shivered. Mike ripped open the robe. The belt came loose and dropped to the floor. Mike stared.

"Mike," Carla whispered, "don't look at me as if I'm some kind of slave, some kind of machine you've rented. I'm somebody, too."

"Sure," he said. "Fat Joe's hired whore."

"You don't understand. You've got it all wrong, I swear."

She caught her breath and shadows moved along nude, creamy skin. Darkness turned warm and tawny with the slim perfection of her legs. Smoothness softened the slender flatness of her stomach. She breathed deeply, her breasts moving, trembling.

"I'll stick to my part of the bargain," he said. "You handle yours. I intend to stay and enjoy myself. Is that all right?"

"Of course, Mike."

"Did Fat Joe tell you to be nice?"

"Yes. You know he did."

"And you always do what you're told?"

"Mike, don't say it that way. Didn't you hear me? I'm a person. I'm a person, just like you or Holly or anybody."

Her voice shook, trailing off. She turned and suddenly, with a little wriggling motion, she slipped out of the robe. It fell away from her shoulders, crumbling into a soft heap on the floor. With her back to him, she lifted her hands and loosened her hair. The coils came free, flowed silkily over her smooth bare shoulders.

The naked curve of her hips dipped at her narrow waist. She moved gracefully, turning as she went down on the bed. Blue light rippled. She stretched. "Mike," she said. "I don't want to fight. Do you?"

"No," he said. "Not now."

He went to her. She knew what to do. Her mouth was hot, the tip of her tongue a flicker of flame darting. Time twisted with the fluid movement of her supple body but, for a while, he had the feeling of being apart, of being a spectator to this accomplished love gambol.

In the dark glistening of her hair on the pillow, the taut arching of her back, the deep bliss crying, a soft moan breathing with that last yielding surrender, he touched the dark warm wet whirlpool of mocking memory, the knowing that Holly was no better than Carla and he was no better than either one of them. Grab, take what you could get. As Holly had said, nobody cries for a loser. To hell with it. You only live once.

Mike tightened his arms. Thinking spun down, hardness melting with the begging shudder of her loins. She hugged her arms around his neck. Her breath quickened. The firm softness of her breasts sought his lips, his hands, crushed seekingly into his sweaty chest.

"Mike, hold me. Tighter. Please, Mike." Her voice shivered. Her legs thrashed. Her hips rolled and bucked.

Darkness cloaked the burst of clinging, supersweet climax. She pushed her hands up, digging her fingers into the tangle of his hair. The hard kissing of her mouth pleaded for hurt.

Then suddenly, tiredly, she relaxed. Turning, she touched his face. With the movement, Mike held an instant of flatness. Love by the numbers. The expert. He took a deep breath. Exhaustion made him feel that he had nothing left to give.

Minutes passed before either spoke or moved. Then she smiled.

"Was I nice, Mike?"

"You ought to know, expert."

"Oh, Mike."

"Don't play games. For you, it's all in a night's work."

"No," she whispered and then, later, when they were drinking, she kept saying he didn't understand. "You don't, Mike."

"Okay."

She shook her head helplessly. They smoked cigarettes. They had several more drinks. Once, outside, below the window on the road, there was a fight. Voices cursed. The police siren wailed. Later, getting drunk, curling around, huddling, the splendid pastel of her luxuriant figure curving nakedly, Carla put her head in Mike's lap. Softly, clinging, she whispered his name.

"Mike."

"Yes."

"Listen to me."

"All right, Carla."

"I'm going to tell you something. I love you."

"No," he said thickly. "Don't lie. Don't keep lying."

"Does everything have to be a lie?" She motioned for him not to answer. "Maybe it doesn't matter. If I died right here there wouldn't be anyone to cry even one tear."

"Fat Joe?"

"God damn him," Carla whispered.

"I thought you two were pals."

"Oh, Mike," she said brokenly. "You know better than that. I hate the lousy sight of him. The slob." She shivered. "And don't think you have to tell me anything about him. When I think of ugliness I think of the dirty things he's made me do."

"It's a free country, Carla."

"No, Mike, you're wrong. It isn't a free country for me." She moved, pressing against him and then slowly, the words coming raggedly, she said, "I suppose it's all my fault. Maybe that's why I never wanted to tell you before —" Her voice broke. "I wanted to have you believe in me. I really did, Mike, but it didn't work out.

Fat Joe was always the boss. He never meant for me to marry you but it was real to me, Mike. All those days when you were on top and we were engaged—they were the best days. I was happy. For a little while I even forgot."

"Forgot what?"

"Do you really want to know?"

"Yes," Mike said. "Tell me, damn it. Go ahead, tell me."

"All right." Her voice now low but steady, she chronicled how she had been born and brought up in Detroit. "Nobody mistreated me. My mother and father got divorced but I was no worse off than thousands of other kids. In fact, when I went to live with my sister in Pontiac, I had everything I wanted. At sixteen, I didn't have a worry in the world and don't ask me why I wanted to think I had fallen in love with a man twice my age. I just did. When Jerry married me, I thought I was on Cloud Nine. Well, I wasn't. When we moved down south where his people lived, I found out I was to be treated like a slut. A kitchen girl. An animal to be harnessed and beaten and sometimes to be a receptacle for bestial lust."

A moment passed.

"Mike?"

"I'm listening, Carla."

"Do you know what loneliness is like?"

"I guess so."

"No," she whispered. "I don't think you do. Not the kind that makes living into emptiness. That comes with no friends and nobody to keep you from being hurt. Well, that was my loneliness. Jerry's mother and sister hated me. His father was the sheriff of the county. He wanted big things for his boy. It didn't matter that Jerry was in his thirties. He was still his father's boy. I was a tramp to the man—all women were tramps. One night, when he was drunk, he raped me. Jerry caught him but the old man shouted him down. After that Jerry took his shame out on me. He whipped me. A million times he beat me so I'd say I had teased his father into doing what he did. I wouldn't and one night when he took his belt off to beat me again, I hit him with a beer bottle he had left on the dresser. When he fell, he struck his head. He died right there."

"You killed him."

"Yes," she whispered. "I killed him. Mike, I was only seventeen. I was scared, afraid of what his father would do. I stole what money there was in the house and ran away." She hesitated. "Mike, believe me. I was just a scared kid. I couldn't go back home." She moved her hand helplessly. "Oh, hell, after a while I met Fat Joe. He put tracers on me—and made me go to work. You know what kind of work. And I can't stop now. Joe could have me sent back to face a murder trial tomorrow."

"Wasn't it self-defense?"

"Yes."

"Maybe you could win."

"No, Mike. Not now. Not after years as a call girl." She put her hands over her face. "Oh, God," she whispered. "You were the only decent thing that ever happened to me." She lifted, touching her lips to his. "Mike," she said softly. "I love you."

"I believed that once."

"It's true, Mike."

"You make a lie sound good, Carla."

"No," she moaned. She twisted, moving against him. "Mike, don't say things like that. Please," she begged. "I need you. I love you. You're all I want in this whole wide world." Her lips trembled. "I don't care about Fat Joe or anybody else. Take me away somewhere, Mike. Don't let me be hurt any more. I'll be good for you. I swear it, Mike."

Mike shook his head.

"Carla," he said. "It's too late."

She curved to him, her lips parted, the shimmering blackness of her hair falling softly over her bare shoulders Her lovely, full breasts looked at him.

"Mike."

"Yes."

"I love you."

He said, "Oh, Christ."

"Wait." She drew him down. The warmth of her pressed sleekly. Her lips kissed his mouth. She turned her head. Her fingers traced sparks on his torso. She said, "Let me show you, Mike. It's never too late."

CHAPTER TEN

THE TELEPHONE in the hotel room rang shrilly. Mike opened his eyes. A slant of morning sunshine streaked across the foot of the bed. He kicked back the covers, sitting up, rubbing his face, running his fingers through his hair. From the bathroom came the splash of bathwater.

"Mike!"

Carla's voice jerked him wide awake but, for one last moment, in himself, he waited and then, like watching parts of a jigsaw puzzle falling into place, he remembered drinking, arguing, loving. On the bedside table, beside the blue-shaded lamp, the empty fifth and two glasses glinted coldly. Lipstick-stained cigarette butts littered the ashtrays. Mike squeezed his eyes shut. His head held a little man beating with a pointed hammer. The telephone rang again.

"Mike. Don't answer it. I'll answer."

He swung his legs over the edge of the bed and reached for the instrument. The bathroom door opened. Carla had a white towel wrapped around her. It covered her to the breasts, fell to the curve of her hips. Her long bare legs were wet. Water dripped to the carpet.

"Mike," she said swiftly. "Give it to me." Light shifted. She walked to where he was sitting and then, as Mike spoke into the telephone, she leaned down. Her voice trembled. "Who is it?"

"It's not Fat Joe."

Carla let out her breath.

"Well?"

"It's for me." Mike paused and then, speaking into the telephone again, he said, "Okay, Mig. How did you know I was here and what do you want?"

"Are you alone?"

"No, Mig, I'm not alone."

"Carla?"

"Good God, Mig," Mike said. "This is one hell of a time to start asking questions."

"It's after nine, Mike."

"Okay—I slept late."

"With her?"

"Listen," Mike grunted, "that's my business."

Mig said, "I guess you're right. Anyway, when I saw you going to the hotel last night, I didn't need any second sight to know where you were heading." She paused. "But I didn't call to pry, Mike. Holly telephoned. She had an idea you were at the Blue Gull last night. She also had the idea you might have come back here to my place with me. I let her know she was wrong about us, but I told her I'd do my best to locate you."

"Thanks, Mig."

"That's all right." Mig stopped and then, going on again, she said, "I'm off until this evening. If you have time, come over."

"Okay, Mig. I may do that."

Mike put down the telephone and then, quickly, lying a little, saying Jake needed him at the fuel dock, Mike started to get dressed. Carla sat down on the edge of the bed and crossed the bare legs. The towel hid exactly nothing.

"Mike, do you really have to go?"

"Yes."

"When can you get back?"

"I don't know."

"Today?"

"I said I didn't know."

He looked away from her and buttoned his shirt. He stuffed it into his pants and then, after turning to the dresser and running a comb through his hair, he put his wallet into his hip pocket and tightened his belt. As he did, Carla stood up. Little drops of moisture glittered on her long dark lashes. She had all the lusciousness of ripe fruit. The towel slipped. Light glistened on naked hips.

"Mike."

"Don't make it any harder, Carla."

"I love you."

"We're too old to kid each other."

She shook her head. "I'm not joking and I'm not lying. As God is my witness, I'm telling the truth." She moved to him, lifting her hands, slipping her arms around his neck. Pressing hard, hugging up, she kissed his mouth passionately. Then, letting go, turning her head a little, she whispered. "No matter what happens, I'm not going back to Joe Nicca. Never Mike. During the night, I made up my mind. If you want to go ahead and tell all you know about him, I won't say a word against you—I won't try to make it look as if you attacked Ted Adam."

"Really? Joe might object."

"I don't care."

"No, Carla," Mike said. "To hell with it. Let him have his way. Be sensible."

"I am, Mike. For once I'm being sensible and whenever you want me, I'll be right here, waiting."

Walking back toward old Jake's place in the dusty glare of the bright sun, Mike could not separate truth from lies. From past experience, he knew Carla was capable of saying anything. She could very well be lying. That was her history. Why should he believe her? Once burned, he thought, twice shy. Damn it, he must have been out of his mind to get involved with her again.

Trouble with a capital T. Hell's bells, he had known that when he had first crawled into her bed.

Mike lit a cigarette. Maybe that was life. Everything you ever did was a link in a chain. You never escaped the past. He took a deep drag and flipped the cigarette into the dirty slough water. To hell with Carla. Fat Joe too. All that was over and done with and they didn't need to worry about any newspaper stories.

To hell with the newspapers, too. Let somebody else do the dirty work. He got off the shoulder to let a truck pass. It jolted in the ruts, kicking up a cloud of dust. Behind it, two cars full of Mexicans and their fishing and picnic gear headed toward the breakwater. A little black-eyed girl waved a flower at Mike and squealed happily.

Mike lifted his hand. A few minutes later, cutting down the bank, he took the path around the back of the collapsing cannery. A flock of swamp ducks and black coots paddled in the weedy shallows where he had found Ted. Mike looked just once. That was over, too. Forget it. Only it wasn't that easy. He was part of Ted's existence because he was part of Holly's. Sure, Carla said she wanted him. But so did Holly. The breath of Holly was the beat of a drum. Let Ted be dying. Let everything else go to hell. Holly, Holly! You crazy bastard, he thought, stop it. But when he got to the house, going out to the back porch to meet her, he knew there could be no stopping.

"Holly?"

She turned, standing with her back to the railing. Behind her the sun glared on the harbor. A sport boat headed out. In the crowd of fishermen that jammed the rails, a woman laughed shrilly. The sound lifted over the steady chugging of the engine. Gulls dipped, squawking. A gust of wind caught the yellow circle of Holly's house dress. It fluttered up against her tanned legs. Sex. The word fitted every smooth curve. She lifted her hand, holding her blond ponytail against the breeze for a moment. Sex. Mike held his breath. Heat hammered the rim of his mind. Even after a night with Carla, he could not look at Holly without thinking nakedness, without feeling satin sleekness across her hips, the burning touch of her tongue. Love? No, just sex; ripe, lush, sensual sex. Honest to God, he could taste her, feel every inch of her, remember each purring shudder. Maybe he was wrong. Maybe that was love. At least it had reality. It was not something you talked about but could not understand or touch. He took a step toward her. A swift warmth flooded her eyes but when he lifted his hands, reaching for her, she shook her head warningly.

"Don't, Mike."

"Why?"

She turned her head a little.

"Jake's down on the dock. He could look up and see us."

"To hell with Jake."

"No, Mike."

"Do you know what I want?"

She waited.

"Yes," she said finally. "I know." Then quickly she changed the subject. "Monty was here again."

"Is that why you got me back here?"

"Yes."

"To hell with Monty."

"He's not just another dumb cop, Mike."

"I never said he was." Mike paused, studying his cigarette. "All right," he went on finally, "what did he want this time? Does he still think I shoved Ted into the slough?"

"Don't joke." Holly put her hands together, looking down at her locked fingers. "Monty has been talking to a man named Joe Nicca."

"Oh, God."

"Do you know him?"

"Yeah," Mike said. "He is the world's greatest son of a bitch. He was my manager and front man for the gambling syndicate that had my contract. Where did Monty see Joe?"

"At the hotel."

"That's fine," Mike said bitterly. He inhaled, blew out the smoke in twin angry streams. "Well, what did Joe have to say?"

"That at one time you tried to kill him."

"Well," Mike said softly, "he's right about that. When they let me know what kind of a screwing I'd taken, I went after Joe. If I hadn't been slugged with the butt of a gun, I'd have pounded that fat bastard to death." Mike stopped. "To hell with it. That's done."

"Then why is this Joe Nicca here?"

"He figures I can hurt him." Dragging at the cigarette, Mike explained how it was possible that he could pull the string on Joe. "But damn it," Mike said viciously, "I don't want any part of any of it. I'm not going to do any talking." He stopped again and then, when Holly asked why he didn't go to Joe and tell him there wasn't going to be any trouble, Mike shook his head helplessly. "He wouldn't believe me. Like everybody else, he judges by himself. He is a liar, so he figures I'm a liar. His best bet is to set me up for a load of grief and then make a deal."

"Mike," Holly whispered, "I'm afraid."

Before he could answer, old Jake came wheezing up from the fuel dock. Business was slow. The fishing fleet had moved north to Eureka. It didn't look as if there would be a raise. Expenses were eating up the profit. Ted's accident was costing a small fortune. Jake rambled on, neither Mike nor Holly answering or even listening.

Later in the morning, when Jake went hunching back down to fuel a small cabin cruiser, Mike found himself getting into a nagging fuss with Holly. It was all questions and answers. Did Joe Nicca have money? Hell, yes. People with money could do anything. All right. If they had money, they wouldn't have to worry about people like Joe or anybody else. Yes, Holly was right about that. Maybe Ted would die; old Jake, too. Damn it, everybody died but it could take a long time. Why not take a chance the way other people did and have each other? No. That wasn't enough for her. Did he know old Jake was worth a hundred thousand or more? Yes, Mike knew. What the hell good did that do? She told him not to swear. The railing on the float was rotten. Yes, Mike knew that, too. Was she hinting at murder? Oh, for God's sakes, Mike, stop talking madness. All right, what the hell did she mean?

"Don't yell at me," Holly said. She clenched her hands, changing the subject suddenly, asking where he had spent the night. "That pink-headed cocktail waitress said that you weren't at her place. I suppose she lied?"

"No," Mike said. "I wasn't with Mig."

"But you were with a woman?"

Mike stared at her.

"All right. Would it matter?"

Holly shrugged carelessly. The low neckline of her dress left her shoulders bare and showed a softness like pale gold. The thrust of her breasts breathed up but then, angrily, instead of answering him, she asked another question.

"Was it that Carla woman?"

Mike flipped away his cigarette.

"Was it?" Holly insisted.

"Yes," Mike said suddenly. "I sure as hell wasn't doing any good around here."

"So you went somewhere else?"

"Have it your way."

"Was she nice?"

"Oh, hell," Mike swore. "Figure it out for yourself."

The fight ended there because Jake came shambling up again. He was hungry. Telling him she would get lunch right way, Holly started in Pa this and Pa that. Mike could not stand it. The whole damn world was nothing but angles and false-faced lies. Money. His guts ached with the word. Then the beat came back. Holly, Holly, Holly. Oh, God, what is she doing to me?

He felt sick with a kind of thick, crazy desire but, to keep from ending up in another hopeless argument, Mike walked out of the house.

In front of the Blue Gull, he stopped to talk to a couple of old friends, fishermen who had known his father. After a moment, as usual, the conversation veered around to Mike's ring career. He did not want to talk about it. After refusing an offer of a drink, he cut around behind the bait store, walking down the narrow dirt alley toward the rooms where Mig lived.

A gang of kids passed. One of them had a little transistor radio pressed to his ear. The music faded. They disappeared around the side of a rotting old warehouse. By an overflowing garbage can, a runty black dog sniffed. Mike located Mig's place and started up by the back door. The steps creaked. In the first-floor apartment, a TV squawked. A fat woman in a sloppy pink bathrobe came out and tossed a beer bottle toward the garbage can in the yard. Glass shattered. The woman cursed the dog and went back inside. Mike stopped on the warped landing. A shadow moved behind the kitchen window curtain. He knew Mig had seen him, but he rapped anyway.

CHAPTER ELEVEN

MIG WAS just leaving.

"Damn," she said. "Just a little while after I called you at the hotel, Herb telephoned."

"Who?"

"My ex-husband. I don't want to see him."

"Okay," Mike said. "What do we do?"

Mig got her car. It was a little foreign job, white, with bucket seats. Noon brightness glared on the windshield. Light fringed her pink hair. Her lipstick and her dress were pink too. As she shifted gears, heading out toward the highway bridge, her skirt pulled up over her knees. Nylon glistened smoothly.

"Nice."

"Me or the car?"

Mike grinned.

"Both."

They crossed the bridge. A couple of kids were perched on the rail, fishing with hand lines. At the stop, traffic passed, tailing a big truck. On the slope above the highway, smoke trailed away from the tall stack at the chemical plant.

"Santa Cruz, Mike?"

"Suit yourself."

She turned left. It was her day off. The car picked up speed. The needle moved to sixty-five. Mike lit a pair of cigarettes and passed one to her. She took a deep drag, breathing out the smoke, plucking a speck of tobacco from her lips with the tip of her tongue.

"Mig," Mike asked. "How about Herb?"

"That bastard."

"Is it that bad?"

"Yes."

"I thought a divorce ended everything."

"No, Mike. Once you marry somebody, you never really get free. Even without the memories, there is always some damned little thing tying you together." She paused. "Forget it, Mike. I know you didn't come to talk about me or my troubles."

"How do you know?"

"Feminine intuition."

"Is there such a thing?"

"Because I'm a smart girl, then."

Mike leaned back without answering. He watched the white line, the quick flash of passing traffic. The highway curved up over the crest of an oak-dotted hill.

"Is it a woman, Mike?"

"What do you think?"

"Holly?"

"Yes," Mike said softly. "Holly."

Later, in a small waterfront bar, Mike clammed up. What could he say? Whiskey sandpapered his throat. He chain-smoked. The girl I want—she's after an old man's money. For all I know, she'd kill to get it. No, for Christ's sake, he couldn't say that. An old man dies easy. All it would take was a little push, a broken rail, a big gulping lungful of water. No, damn it, he couldn't say that. Holly had never put it into so many words. Maybe she really did love old Jake. A hundred thousand dollars. What the hell, it was only money. Now, wouldn't that be a sweet thing to say to Mig? Or maybe he could tell Mig about the way Holly looked lying naked. He laughed to himself.

"Mike?"

"Yes, Mig."

"Can't I help you?"

"No."

"Why are you so sure?"

"I'm not, Mig."

"You know how I feel about you?"

"I guess so."

"Trust me, Mike."

He made a stab at explaining but it was as if he were picking words from the hard surface of his mind. The real meaning lay underneath. Two or three times, coming close to the truth, he almost broke through. But by early afternoon when they knocked off drinking to eat a steak, he still had not touched reality. Could one woman be everything? No, that wasn't what he really wanted to know. Was there any real meaning to life? Did it matter one hoot in hell whether you cheated or didn't cheat; whether you counted all the marbles and always gave the right change? Was that sucker bait? Look at Fat Joe. He did all right. Money never hurt him. Oh, Jesus, that wasn't it either. Somebody was going to get old Jake's money. As Holly said, nobody lived forever.

A hundred thousand dollars.

So close.

So damned close. His hands sweated. Money. It made you big.

"Mike?"

He forced a grin.

"I'm sorry, Mig."

"Get it off your chest. I wasn't kidding. I want to help."

"Sure."

They went back to drinking. He still could not make sense out of what he was trying to say. Lights blurred. A whole day shot to hell. He got that big feeling, the emptiness of those lonely months after he had hit the skids. Broke? He knew all about that. They changed bars. In the car, Mig slipped around, lifting her face. He kissed her mouth. She clung to him. He slid his hand up her leg. She pressed hard against his fingers and then they were at a bar where they could watch the Santa Cruz wharf. The world tipped. Glass glittered.

"Mike," Mig said. "I love you."

Not again. Not from her, too.

"Don't, Mig."

"It doesn't matter how you feel toward me. It's what I feel. Right there in the car, you could have had me."

"You're drunk, Mig."

"No."

They argued. The bar filled up. At one end, a gang of college kids started slapping time on the bar and singing folk songs. A mug of beer got spilled. A plump blond came from one of the booths, shouldering her way to the ladies' room. On the way back, she stopped.

"Honey," she said to Mike. "I know you."

"Sure."

The blond blinked.

"Honey," she went on finally. "Your girl friend has got pink hair."

"I know."

"Honey, that ain't right."

"Okay."

The blond nodded, swaying and then, after saying again that she knew Mike, she pursed her red lips thoughtfully. The low cut of her blue dress dipped across the huge curves of her breasts. Her escort, a heavyshouldered fellow with crewcut straw hair came over to collect her but she shrugged his hand off her shoulder.

"I've got it," she said suddenly. "Mike Shannon, the fighter."

"Okay," Mig broke in. "So you win the booby prize. Now let us alone."

"Honey," the blond said thickly, "I already told you that you have pink hair so don't get so goddamned smart."

"Go away," Mig said.

The blond slapped Mig. Mig waited a moment, touching the tips of her fingers to her cheek. Then, casually she picked up her glass and poured her drink down the front of the blond's dress. Wet splotched cloth, soaking, dripping down the blond's legs. Her escort knocked the glass out of Mig's hand and then took a roundhouse swing at the seated Mike.

Blocking the blow, Mike slid to his feet. He hit twice; a left to the middle, a right cross to the jaw. The big fellow staggered back, fell over a table. A bottle hit the mirror. One of the college kids jumped up on the bar. The bartender slugged him across the shins with a broom handle. A woman screamed. Mig took Mike's hand. At the front the college kids were going for the bartender but Mig led Mike to the rear. Behind the bar, a door opened. Mig's high heels clicked on the cement. A police siren shrieked in the street. They crossed the dark parking lot and got into her car.

"Mig," Mike said. "You're a genius."

"Remember? I work in a bar, Mike. There's a trick to every trade. One of them is always to know where the back door is located. That's second nature with me."

They stopped twice during the return to Slat Landing. They drank some more and they danced. Mig kissed with her arms locked around his neck. Her mouth tasted of alcohol. The tip of her tongue burned hard and deep. She moved her round, high hips smoothly under his hands and, later, at her place, going up to the door after they had put the car away, she trembled under the touch of his fingers. The steps creaked. A drift of night fog misted in her pink hair. In the house across the alley, the bluish tube-glow of TV made a flickering moon. In one of the apartments below Mig's place, a man and a woman were arguing. The voices blurred indistinctly. Mig opened her purse and fumbled for her key.

There was a bottle in the kitchen cupboard and ice in the refrigerator. She told Mike to mix drinks while she got into something more comfortable. He lit a cigarette. Whiskey gurgled, splashing. The room slanted. Under the faucet at the sink, he loosened the cubes in the ice tray. Water dripped. An ice cube dropped to the floor. He kicked it under the table. In the tiny living room, Mig put a record on her hi-fi. Mike walked to the doorway. Mig looked up. Except for high heels, she was wearing only a filmy flesh-colored negligee. It hid nothing. Light from the lamp silhouetted the slim curves of her boyish hips. The pink nipples of her high firm breasts jutted.

"Like me?"

"The end of a perfect day."

"No," she whispered. "Don't say it as if it doesn't matter, Mike. You think I'm cheap? You think I'm crazy?"

"No, Mig."

She came close. The robe was tied loosely. There wasn't a thing he could not see. It was all nice. It was all his. The words were in her eyes. She looked up and even when she took her drink she kept staring at him. Her lips parted.

"Mike."

"Yes?"

"I'm shameless. I may not be cheap, but I have no shame, not with you. I don't care. Love can't do anything wrong. I've waited all my life. Even when I was married, I was waiting, Mike. I want to belong to you."

"We're drunk, Mig."

"No. Even if we were, though, it wouldn't matter. All day you've been talking to me and saying nothing. You're worried about Ted. You don't know if he fell or got pushed, if he'll live or die. You have that Holly in your head. You want something but you think it's wrong. Oh, don't argue, Mike. Maybe I've got things mixed up. Maybe you weren't really trying to say any of those things but I'll tell you what I'm saying. I love you."

"I'm not worth it."

"That hasn't got anything to do with what I feel. Even if you hated me, it wouldn't matter. When I was a little girl, I loved you.

Through high school, it was the same. When you went away, I was happy for you but I cried for myself. The night of your last fight, I bawled myself to sleep. Now you're back. Be nice, Mike. Give me a chance. Don't you see? I know what I want. It's right for me. I'm not afraid."

"Mig."

He said her name softly. How would it be with her? Good? Honest? At least she was a girl who did not pretend, who did not need to pretend. A guy could forget with her. To hell with money. To hell with getting. He watched her turn to put her glass down. Nylon swirled against her sleek legs. She walked toward the bedroom. At the doorway, she paused, looking back.

"Mike."

"Yes, Mig."

"Be good to me."

He was. As good as possible, that is. It was not really fair. Carla had tired him, emptied him.

CHAPTER TWELVE

NEXT MORNING dawned gray and foggy. The fuel dock dripped moisture. When Mike got up, his bunk smelled damp. He cooked breakfast and shaved. While he was smoking a cigarette over a mug of steaming coffee, Holly came down from the house.

"Good morning, Mike."

"Coffee?"

She walked into the shack and got up on the stool. Grayish light shimmered in her hair. In sandals, a yellow skirt, a white blouse, she looked like a kid but when she spoke again there was an adult chagrin in her voice.

"You didn't come back yesterday?"

"No," Mike said.

"Why?"

"I didn't feel like arguing."

Holly stared.

"Mike," she said, "Where did you go?"

"Santa Cruz."

"Alone?"

"No," Mike said.

He turned, taking the pot from the hot plate. Steam clouded up as he poured coffee for her. He gave her a cigarette and thumbed his lighter. She crossed the tanned legs, leaning to get the light. The flickering glow moved tawny lights over the satin sleekness of her. Under the skirt and blouse she was naked. Mike's hand trembled. The drum started to beat. He turned to glance out through the misty window. In the channel, an open skiff with an outboard motor was passing. The sound of the fog horn on the breakwater drifted through the fog.

"Mike, were you with Mig?"

He faced her again. He waited.

"Well?"

He decided quickly to lie.

"We had a few drinks."

"We?"

"Yes," Mike said. "Mig and I."

"Is that all?"

"Yes."

Holly sipped her coffee.

"What's the matter," she asked finally. "Doesn't Mig like it?"

"Like what?"

"Oh, you know damned well." Holly put down the mug. "Mike," she said suddenly, "Herb Sanky was nosing around here yesterday."

"Herb?"

"Mig's ex-husband."

"So?"

"He knew you were out with Mig." Holly put the mug down on the desk and squashed her cigarette out. "Herb is big. He's built like you. And he's a mean bastard."

"Don't swear."

"What could he be after?"

Holly stood up. Swiftly, emphasizing her words by moving her hands, she described Herb. He was a bulky, dark-haired guy with a skinny face, a mechanic with a San Francisco diesel company.

"They supply a lot of equipment to the fishing fleet," Holly said. "Herb comes down here on service calls several times a month. He and Ted are friends—but, Mike, let me tell you something. Herb is the kind of nasty, jealous hot-head likely to do anything."

"Okay," Mike said. "I believe you."

"I'm worried."

"Why?"

"We don't want any trouble."

"Is that all that's bothering you, Holly?"

"No."

"Are you jealous?"

"Yes," she whispered. "I am. I'm jealous as can be."

She walked to Mike. He moved his coffee things aside and put his hands on her slim waist. She pushed closer, brushing against him. His fingers slid over the smooth curve of her hips. Under the thin material, she was nakedly sleek.

"Do you know what I want?"

"Yes, Mike."

"Is that what you want?"

"Yes."

"When will you marry me?"

"Mike, we've been over that. We've got to wait."

"For Ted and old Jake to die."

"Don't say it that way, Mike."

"All right," he said harshly. "Does it sound better to say we're waiting to get our hands on Jake's money?"

"I'm being good to him."

"Sure, for a shot at a hundred thousand dollars."

"All right. I like money." Holly put her hands on Mike's arms. Her fingers squeezed. Under her dress, the firm mounds of her breasts breathed up. She parted her lips. "Don't be a fool," she whispered. "We could live our whole lives without getting another chance like this. Be honest, Mike. You like money, too."

"I like something else better."

"You can wait."

"Can I?"

"You'll have to, Mike."

"Don't be so sure of yourself, Holly. There are other women."

"Carla?"

"She's one."

"Mig?"

"All right," Mike said heavily. "Mig too."

A moment passed.

"Mike," Holly said finally. "I haven't got any hold on you."

"No. I know it."

"If you don't want to wait until we can be married, you don't have to."

"I know that, too."

"Well?"

"Damn it, Holly. You know how I feel."

"You want me?"

"Yes."

"You won't go away?"

"No," Mike said, after a moment.

"You won't be sorry. I love you."

"But you love money more."

"Mike," Holly whispered, "don't be so stubborn. I want everything you want. I have feelings, same as you. Waiting is just as hard for me. I want to be in your arms. Oh, God, Mike, sometimes I can hardly bear thinking of you down here in the shack. You know what I need—and I know what you need—but while things are as they are, we've got to be careful. To Jake, Ted is a fine son. Jake expects me to be faithful. I'm all Jake has to hang on to right now, with Ted in a hospital fighting death. I have to live the way Jake wants me to live."

"That might go on for years. You don't know how long Jake will last."

"True."

"What the hell am I supposed to do?"

"Wait. I'm waiting. I feel that it won't be too long."

"You do?'

She stirred in his arms. The tips of her breasts crushed. The warmth of her legs burned against Mike. The pale slant of gray light glistened in her honey-gold hair. Shadows slanted the smooth planes of her cheeks and darkened the red curve of her full parted lips. For the space of a single stripped moment, opening her eyes wide, she let him see memory pooled blue, the hot yielding waiting and he remembered the taut lift of her back, the crying twist in the scalding flow of melting surrender. Holly. Holly! The beat of her name pounded, a hard thrust of pain. His hands held heat and without touching more or letting him kiss her mouth, she made his wanting a savage hunger.

"Mike—"

"Yes, Holly."

"I'll make everything worthwhile."

"When?"

"Soon."

"How soon?"

"As soon as I can."

She broke away from him.

A little later, Jake came shuffling down to the fuel dock, gumming his pipe, blinking, puttering. Mike sold a couple of five-gallon cans of gasoline to a man and a woman in a skiff. Holly scolded the old man for coming out in the fog.

"You've got to take care of yourself, Pa."

"I'm all right." He blinked and rubbed his gnarled knuckles across his eyes. "Outside of being a little dopy with them pills, I feel fine."

"I worry about you."

"I'm all right, Holly."

"Don't get near the railing. You could easily fall off this float."

Mike heard that while he was ringing up his sale on the cash register. He closed the drawer and wiped his hands on a rag he carried in his hip pocket. Stepping outside to where Holly was standing with Jake, Mike said he guessed Jake knew his way around the float pretty well.

"That's right," Jake said toothlessly. He puffed his pipe, tipping his hat, squinting into the fog. "But its mighty nice to have somebody who cares, Mike."

"Yeah."

"Ted's got to get well. He's got to make it."

"He will, Jake."

When it was getting toward noon, Holly took the old man to the house so she could start getting his lunch. The two of them climbed slowly up the rickety steps. A gust of wind caught the circle of Holly's skirt and it flared up against her thighs. Mist dripped on worn wood. The old man stumbled. She braced him. At the top he stopped to catch his breath and then, turning, blinking, looking back down to where Mike stood on the float, Jake muttered about the sleeping pills he was taking for his nerves.

"By God, they get me dizzy."

Holly hooked her hand through the crook of his arm.

"You'll be all right, Pa."

" 'Course I will." Jake grinned and gummed his pipe. "Long as I got you and Mike on the place, I know I ain't got nothing to worry about."

CHAPTER THIRTEEN

AFTER DARK when he had closed up for the night, Mike went up to the house. He managed to talk to Holly alone for a few minutes but then, shirtless, his long underwear buttoned up to his scrawny throat, his skimpy gray hair dull under the glare of the light, Jake came out to the kitchen. He filled a cup with hot coffee, drinking it noisily, mumbling along about Ted. He made it sound as if Ted was everything good wrapped up in one package but, finally, going clear through the trip to the hospital, Jake got off on how bad times were getting. Disjointedly, he complained about business, about the slow fishing season. Lighting his pipe, he went on, ranting against taxes and the way the government always had its hand out.

"It's getting so it don't matter how hard a man works. He still ends up with nothing."

"Well," Mike said, "it's a hell of a sight better here than in most countries."

"Guess so."

"You sure wouldn't have anything in Russia."

Jake puffed his pipe angrily.

"By God," he muttered. "I know that. But it wouldn't hurt to cut taxes once in a while."

"Everything costs money."

"Sure," Jake said. "But it don't look like they'd take so much from people like me. Hell, they got big business to collect from. The big ones are getting all the gravy. Look at us. Pumping oil. Hell, I ain't even going to be able to give you a raise."

"You own property."

"Sure I do. A few hundred feet of slough waterfront. I'm property poor. Taxes all the damned time." Jake lifted his cup. His old wrinkled hand shook. "Sometimes, a man gets to feeling money ain't nothing but trouble."

"A lot of people feel that way. A lot of people don't."

Jake drained his cup. A spill of coffee trickled down his chin. He wiped it away with the back of his hand. A drip splotched on his underwear. He blinked, pushing away his cup and saucer. Breathing heavily, grunting, he got a match out of his pants pocket and scratched it under the table. The flame burned yellowishly. He touched it to his pipe. His cheeks sucked in and out. Smoke puffed. He shook out the match and then went right back to swearing about the government.

"Taxes."

"Somebody has to pay, Jake."

"Hell, they're giving away the money."

"Not to me."

"No," Jake grumbled. "You got to be in some other place to get it. Them fellows in Washington is hellbent to get money to other places."

"That's the cold war," Mike said. "It could be worse. At least when you don't like it, you can complain all you want. This is still the best country in the world. A lot of bad things happen but nobody has to pretend they're right. Anyway, I'll tell you one thing, Jake. I like it here."

"Sure, it's better in our country. But hell, Mike, they got it fixed so somebody always has his hand in a man's pocket. By God, when I was a boy things were different."

"I guess so."

Jake puffed stubbornly.

"No guess to it."

"Well," Mike said. "That was a long time ago."

Jake thought about it, gumming the pipe stem. After a while he said, "You're right, Mike. No reason for me to get all stirred up. A fellow gets to forgetting how the years sneak past him. With Ted laid up and me not knowing if he's going to live or die, it gets me cranky. He's a smart one, too. As I told Monty Gomez, Ted don't have no enemies. People like that boy. The sheriff could poke around forever and he wouldn't find anyone who didn't like Ted." Jake nodded to himself. "But me and Holly get lonely, don't we?"

"Yes, Pa."

"I'm lucky to have you, Holly."

"You keep me from being lonely, Pa."

"Sure. You miss Ted same as me. Well, damn it, if the government don't end up taking everything and sending it overseas some place, you and Ted will have all I've got."

"Who's worrying about that, Pa?"

Jake cackled, weirdly amused. "I know you're not studying about me passing on, Holly. I was just setting things straight in your mind. Of course, I been extra shaky taking these pills. Sometimes they fix me so I can't get hold of myself but I don't figure to need them much longer. I never needed anything to make me sleep before. In fact, if you remember, up until Ted's trouble I was getting around here pretty good."

"Pa, it doesn't hurt to be careful. Watch yourself on the steps. Don't get too near railings and things."

Jake grinned.

"A woman always fusses."

Holly said, "Somebody has to fuss over you, Pa. Somebody has to care."

Mike looked up. Holly did not bat an eye. If she did not mean what she was telling the old man, she sure as hell was a good actress. She even managed to look plain and motherly. Pouring Jake more coffee, giving his cheek a little warm pecking kiss, she gave no hint of not being absolutely sincere in everything she was saying. Even to Mike, at the moment she looked like a subdued worried little wife—kind of pretty, too pretty, but definitely a bungalow type. Finally, because he could not stand listening to her and Jake, Mike got up to go.

Holly walked outside with him.

He waited for her to close the door. The latch clicked. Light through the window misted, blurring in the night fog. A car passed.

"Mike," she said.

"I'm listening."

"Don't be upset."

"I hate to see you lie to that old man."

"I'm keeping him happy. Is that bad? Besides, we're the ones who matter, Mike."

He touched her, the tips of his fingers sliding down her bare arms. A wisp of blond hair blew against his cheek.

"You don't seem to have much time for me."

"I will, Mike."

"Tonight?"

She moved still closer, but he dared not embrace her. He breathed the sweet fragrance, the scent of her hair. The red curve of her mouth parted breathlessly. Her eyes held a giving, a hot melting flood of warmth.

"Well?" Mike insisted.

"All right," she whispered. "If I can."

"What time?"

"After midnight."

"That late?"

"We have to be sure Jake is sound asleep."

"Yeah," Mike said bitterly. "I forgot. We wouldn't want to upset the apple cart."

"Please, Mike."

"I'm tired of waiting."

"Please," she begged. "I love you."

"You've told me that."

"It's true."

"You've lied to everybody else. Why not to me?"

"Mike," she moaned.

"When will you leave this and marry me?"

"Not yet."

"When?"

"Please, Mike. It won't be long."

"Until what? Marriage?"

"Until midnight."

Her hips moved. She lifted. Her lips brushed his mouth. The tip of her tongue traced heat.

"I love you."

She shivered and then, swiftly, before he could hold her, she turned and opened the door again. As she did, Jake called.

"Holly?"

"Yes, Pa."

"Maybe you'd like to go out with Mike."

"No."

"You don't have to stay here with me."

"Pa, I want to stay."

The door closed. Faintly, Mike heard the click of Holly's heels going back toward the kitchen. They faded into the mutter of Jake's voice and, suddenly, angrily, Mike started toward the Blue Gull. God damn it, he needed a drink. Truck lights glared. Dirt crunched. The low sound of the fog horn drifted through the mist. He took the path down around the back of the cannery. A rat scuttled into the darkness. Where the path regained the road, Mike saw the hotel, the grocery and bait store and the neon sign of the Blue Gull. Two more cars rattled past. Lights glimmered wetly. Mike lit a cigarette. Holly's last remark came back.

"I want to stay."

Good God.

Lies.

A hundred thousand dollars.

Mike inhaled, hot ash burning red. He blew thin streams of smoke. One woman with two faces. Nineteen. Holly... Holly... Maybe having her was all that really mattered. What else did he want? The question scorched his mind. To hell with it. Wasn't the whole damned world always saying every man had a price? Okay. Holly was his price. Why not? What else did he need? Nothing. Christ, he could forget the bright lights, the smell of success, the way it felt to be a big wheel. Once, after the crash, after the balloon had exploded, when there had been no more good times, no more fights, publicity, no more black-slapping, he had tried to drink himself into the gutter. Nothing left, he had thought. Hell, he had been all wrong. Up until Holly, he had never touched the real edge of living.

He flipped his cigarette to the road, crossed the parking lot. In front of the Blue Gull, beside a parked car, a man and woman were arguing. Wind fluttered a red dress. The woman swore with blunt ugliness. Mike shoved open the tavern door. Cigarette haze—hum of voices—rock-and-roll beat of the juke box; Mike let the door close behind him and then, as he walked to the bar, Mig hurried over to meet him, her hair a pink plume.

"Mike! Oh—good to see you, Mike."

"Hi, Mig."

She waited expectantly.

"Buy you a drink?" he said.

"No."

"Cigarette?"

"All right."

He watched the glow of the lighter reflect in pink hair. She exhaled, tipping up her face. Her black sweater hugged her breasts. Tight black Capri pants snugged her boyish hips but he was seeing her the way she had been with the robe slipping to the floor. Time slanted back. Beside her bed, there had been a lamp. The soft light had darkened with the pulse throbbing in her throat and, afterward, huddling small, her cheeks wet with tears, the taste of salt on her mouth, she had whispered his name.

"Mike."

"Yes."

"Why wasn't it good?"

"You were sweet, Mig."

"Don't fool me."

"Okay, Mig."

"I tried, Mike."

"Forget it, Mig. We've had too much to drink."

"No. Oh, God, Mike, I wanted so much to be good. Not for me but for you. Only there is no pretend in me. It wasn't very much. What did I do wrong?"

"It wasn't you, Mig."

"You've had other girls, Mike. Are they better?"

"Shut up, Mig."

"I can't Mike. Why wasn't it right?"

"I don't know."

"I love you, Mike."

"No."

"You can't stop it from being true, Mike."

"I don't want you hurt."

"That doesn't matter. I love you, hurt or not."

The scene in Mig's room blurred in Mike's eyes. He knew and standing there by the bar, surrounded by drunks, Mig knew too. The night had been a failure. But the day—the day had been good. Mig managed to smile.

"Mike. The ride was fun. Wasn't the ride fun?"

"You bet."

"Santa Cruz."

Mike grinned. "The fight at the bar."

"It seems so long ago, Mike."

"One day."

"No," she said softly, "it's more than that. It's a whole stretch of living." She stopped, frowned. "But that's not what I want to talk to you about. Mike. I was hoping you would call me or come here so I could tell you."

"Tell me what?"

"About Herb."

"Your ex-husband?"

"Yes." Mig paused. "He's crazy jealous. The thing is— he's got a gun, Mike."

"A gun?"

"Yes," Mig whispered. "He won't go away, Mike. He's somewhere around and he's looking for you."

"Me?"

"Yes," Mig said softly. "He's threatening to kill you." Mike laughed.

Time passed. He left the bar after a while, and trudged through sea mists to his shack at the fuel dock.

CHAPTER FOURTEEN

"MIKE?"

"You're late, Holly."

She moved inside the shack. Her skirt swirled. The door creaked, closing behind her. On the desk, the clock pointed to twenty after midnight. In the low glow of the night light fastened to the wall over the head of the bunk, a whiskey bottle glittered. Beside it, on the little working counter by the hot plate, two empty glasses gleamed.

"Don't tell me you've been watching the clock, Mike."

He had been stretched out on the bunk. He rose, and muscles rippled across his bare shoulders. The belt of his khakis cut across the flat of his stomach. He swung his legs over the edge of the bunk and leaned down to squash out his cigarette.

"Yes," he said, "I watched the clock."

"Waiting for me?"

"Who else?"

"Why me? I mean, why is it me you wait for? Why isn't it someone else?"

He shook his head.

"Damned if I know, Holly."

She stared at him.

"I know why."

He said softly, "Yes, maybe you do."

He was staring at her. Gold tints glinted silkily in the ponytailed hair. Christ, she was beautiful. The line of her skirt followed the slim curves of her hips. Darkness slanted the smooth turn of her cheek. She parted her lips. Beneath her white blouse, the high thrust of her breasts breathed. A secret of excitement glistened in her eyes.

"Like me, Mike?"

"I'd be crazy if I didn't."

She moved toward the bunk. Her skirt swayed, swishing back and forth. Lipstick caught light moistly.

"Mike."

"Yes."

"I've been watching the clock too."

"I'll bet."

"Believe me."

"Why, Holly? Why would you be watching clocks?"

"I want you just as much as you want me."

"Don't girls have to be talked into it? Fondled into it? Promoted into it?"

"Not me, Mike."

"You're different."

"I know what I like." Her voice trembled. "You're strong, Mike. But it's not just that. You're able to force me to let go." She paused, lowering her eyes. "Shouldn't I talk that way?"

"I don't know. You're another man's wife."

"I'll be your wife—some day. Meanwhile, I'm your girl."

She lifted her hands, touching him. The tips of her fingers trembled. He felt the thrill. A kind of hot throbbing pulsed in her eyes. Her body shivered and suddenly, breathing raggedly, she squeezed the muscles in his arms.

"Well," she whispered hotly. "I don't care what I say. I'm not a kid. I've seen everything in this world that a man can show a woman. I saw it in the work camps around the lettuce fields. I saw it with Ted whining, begging, crying because he wasn't man enough to make me feel the way he wanted me to feel."

"Don't tell me those things, Holly."

"I want to tell you, Mike. When I was little, I lived in a two-room shanty. I slept out by the stove in the kitchen. I could have been a stray puppy for all anybody cared. Plenty of nights, there was nothing but drunks and sweat and beds squeaking. I've had dirty old men pawing me, poking me." She turned, curling down, her head in his lap. "Oh, hell," she whispered. "Why say it? It's done. Everything is done, Mike. We're the only ones in the whole world who matter. I don't want to remember anything else. Not even Ted." Her voice shivered. "Make me a drink, Mike. Get me drunk. Put your hands on me. Please, Mike. Oh, God, please."

Time crept on. With the door locked, the taste of whiskey in his mouth, the wet touch of her tongue snaking fire between his lips, Mike held bliss captive. The soft warmth of her legs, the sleek sheen of her supple hips, stoked him, lit fires in him. With the fall of her hair loose, the exquisite smoothness of her back yielded to the tightness of his hand.

"Mike."

He moved his mouth against her lips.

"Yes, Holly."

"I love you."

"Sure."

"Do you love me, Mike?"

"I want you."

She shivered, cupping his face in her hands.

"Isn't it more than that, Mike?"

"Does it matter?"

"Yes."

She lifted from him, her breasts trembling, her fingers caught in his hair.

"Say you love me."

"I love you."

"Tell me again, Mike."

"I love you."

"Oh, do love me," she moaned. A shudder rippled through her. Damp, slippery darkness clouded the deepness of surrender; she clung fiercely, hugging. "You bastard. Mike, you beautiful big bastard. Oh, love me, love me, love me…" Silence shivered. He breathed the fragrance of her hair. He held closeness crushed. He loosed her, and kissed each tremulous breast in turn, cupping and squeezing and feeling with his fingers, circling the little alive nipples with his tongue. He stretched up and kissed her lips, tongued her tongue, mouthed her neck, her perfumy ears. He lifted her in his arms, all of her, twisted her around so that his face now was at her feet. He held a warm foot in each hand, stroked the toes with their blood-dyed nails. He kissed the calves, the knees. He stroked the sensitive skin behind the knees, and Holly shivered, Holly gasped. He kissed her thighs, stroking them and feeling them. Her raw nerves, crying for surcease, then broke her. "Mike, I can't stand it. Mike!" And she slapped him, beat her fist against his back and thews. "Ooh… ooh… you lovely bastard, Mike!" Her little fists pounded.

His blood roared like a cataract. He swung her, cradled her. He brought her down across his lap. He lowered her to his bursting pleasure. Sundered like invaded meat, she screamed pain and delight. Deepness whirl-pooled. He breathed the fragrance of her hair. The center of the world exploded and the edge of hurt shuddered, a long moment dark melting. She held on, the flood of warmth a slow yielding.

Later, smoking, drinking, whiskey the breath of her kiss, the night criss-crossing naked shadows, Mike remembered in the slow ache of exhaustion.

Holly. Holly…

Good or bad. Right or wrong.

Christ, it didn't matter.

She pressed against his shoulder.

"Mike?"

"Yes."

"Do you love me?"

"Yes."

"Say it."

"I love you, Holly."

"For always?"

"Yes." Mike said. "For always."

But, right after that, finishing another drink, she would not talk about what was ahead for them.

"Don't ask me."

"Why not?"

"Just don't ask me." She turned, smoking another cigarette. The red glow shimmered the damp sheen of her slender figure. "I just want to be happy. That's all, Mike. Just for once, I don't want to think about anything but just the way it is right here."

"Tomorrow always comes."

"To hell with it."

"It's not that easy, Holly."

"Why?"

"Because I don't want to keep on waiting for you. I don't want to hover here like some damned vulture waiting for a couple of men to die."

"I said I don't want to talk about it."

"Well," Mike said, "I do."

"Don't you want to just lie here and be happy?"

"I wish I could."

Smoke from her cigarette lifted. From outside came the faraway sound of the fog horn. Against the float, water lapped. Somewhere ashore, a dog was barking into the early hours of morning. The ramp creaked, working with the tide. The soft chaffing blended with the steady chugging of a deisel refrigerating engine on the Slat Landing icing dock.

"I just want to know how this possibly can go on," he said.

She inhaled deeply.

"Oh, hell," she said bitterly. She moved her hand, motioning with her cigarette and then, in one of her swift changes of mood, she said, grumbling, thickening her voice, aping the way Jake mushed his words, mimicking him, "Holly, what do you think of Mike? We got to trust somebody. I knew his father. Anyway, I'm lucky. We sure as hell need a man." She laughed. "Well," she whispered. "Did that sound enough like Jake to suit you?"

"You've got him down pat."

"Did you think it was funny?"

"No."

Holly motioned to put her cigarette in the ashtray. "I'm sorry, Mike. I don't want to be serious, but you won't let me forget."

"Forget what?"

"Ted. Jake. Money."

"I guess we don't have much choice," he said.

Holly stiffened.

"What do you mean?"

Mike turned to look at her.

"What's the matter?"

"Nothing."

"You're trembling."

Holly stirred, pushing his hand away.

"I just want to know what you meant?"

"You're sure?"

"Yes."

Mike shrugged.

"Well," he said slowly. "We don't have much choice. We have to make a move."

She let her breath out. "Ah."

"We can't let things drag."

"I'll have to. If I can wait, you can wait."

"Is a chance for Jake's money that important?"

"Yes." Holly stared up into the shadows. "It's really the only thing that is important. We've got each other. We're young. We make each other happy. But look at this dump... Do you think I want to live in something like this?"

"I could do better."

"Sure," Holly whispered. "I know. A paycheck every Friday and a budget to get through the month."

"What's wrong with that?"

"I don't want it."

"Maybe it would be best."

"No," Holly said tensely. "I want to be comfortable. No, don't look at me that way. I'm not crazy. I just want to live so I can do what I want and go where I want. You know what money is, Mike? It's like having life a hundred different ways. All the things people wait for, you can have without waiting. More than that, Mike, you're always right. And when you walk down the street, people hope to God you'll be good enough to notice them. When you want something you get it. Nobody can scare you." She clenched her hands. "I don't want to have to ask somebody else for the things I want to buy. I want the money."

"It's not that good."

"How do you know?"

"Holly, I was up on top for a while."

"Don't you want to be up again?"

"Yes," Mike said. "I won't lie. It's nice to have money in your pocket, Holly. But it isn't everything."

"What is?"

"Nothing, I guess."

"But money is the nearest thing to everything."

"Maybe."

"You just have to have the courage to know what you want."

"All right," Mike said. "I know what I want."

"What?"

"You."

He turned to her and she moved into his arms, slim, lifting, lying across him. The softness of her hair fell over her bare shoulders.

"Mike."

"Yes, Holly."

"I know what I want too."

She moved. Her breasts crushed. Her lips sucked his mouth. The tip of her tongue teased and tickled.

"Mike."

He lifted his arms, digging his fingers into the thickness of her hair. She twisted, huddling, pressing down. Her hands trembled. Her fingers shed flame.

"Mike."

"Yes."

"I love you."

She breathed quickly, hugging. The thick tangle of her hair clenched in his fists. Tawny darkness crouched.

"Mike," she begged again. "Say you love me."

"Holly," he whispered. "I love you. So help me, God. I love you. Sometimes I wish I didn't. It may be all wrong, but I love you."

CHAPTER FIFTEEN

"HEY, MIKE!"

The door creaked. He woke with a start. The hard light of early morning glared on the empty fifth. Inside

the shack, leaning against the edge of the desk, Monty Gomez looked curiously at the two empty glasses. Mike blinked, shoving the covers back and rubbing his hand across his eyes.

"What the hell—"

"Get up, Mike."

"Why?"

"Because," Monty said slowly, "old Jake is dead."

Mike laughed. Monty was trying to set a trap, trying to get a rise out of him.

"Dead," Monty said. "Drowned."

Mike jumped up, swinging his legs over the edge of the bunk. The clock on the desk pointed to fifteen before six. Usually, with boats fueling early, he would have been already up but the habit of early rising did not make getting hold of himself any easier. He felt as if he had been run through a meat grinder.

"Jesus Christ," he said softly. "Monty, you mean it. Jake really is dead."

"Drowned," Monty said again.

"Like Ted almost was," Mike muttered in a strangled voice.

"Are you telling me?"

Mike frowned and reached for a cigarette.

"How the hell could I tell you anything?"

"Can you?"

"No."

Mike stuck the cigarette between his lips. His mouth felt bruised. He knew the pillow was smeared with lipstick. So were butts and one of the glasses. He found his lighter. Flame wavered as his hand shook.

"Nervous, Mike?"

"Give me a chance to wake up."

"This isn't early for you."

"It is this morning."

Mike inhaled. Smoke hit raw in his throat. The stale taste of whiskey soured. The slant of sun dazzling on the water streamed through the window. His eyes stung. Jake dead. Good God, how? Play it smart. Monty could not miss seeing a woman had been in the shack. He sure as hell wouldn't have any trouble guessing. Had he already seen Holly? Mike breathed smoke. Jake dead. Drowned. Okay, let Monty do the talking. He had that look in his eye. That cop look. Well, Mike thought, I sure didn't have anything to do with killing poor Jake.

"Mike, I'm asking you again."

"Yeah, Monty."

"What do you know about this?"

"Nothing. Damn it, I've told you that." Mike frowned. He killed his cigarette, reached for clothes. And he grunted, "Start at the beginning. I want to know about this. Where did you find Jake—and when?"

Monty made it short. He stated that at twenty minutes after five, the *Goshen,* a little cod boat with Dave Short aboard, had passed under the highway bridge. The tide was flooding. Jake's body had been floating face down, snagged on a rotting piling. The sheriff had guessed that Jake had been in the water six or seven hours. There was a bruise on his forehead.

Monty had stopped to wake Holly before descending to the shack. He had left her to get dressed. He meant to talk to her, he told Mike. He should be getting up to the house now. Monty paused, lighting a cigarette for himself. On coming down and before entering the shack, he had inspected the fuel dock, he said. At the rear, behind the shack, the rail was broken. His partner, Art Ting, was stationed outside, at the ramp to see that nothing was touched.

"Okay," Mike said. "So that's where Jake fell."

"If he fell."

"You don't think he jumped?"

"I don't think anything," Monty said. "Not yet." He produced a small notebook and a pencil. While Mike washed and shaved, Monty smoked and asked for an account of the night before. Mike did not lie. It wouldn't have done any good. Monty could guess most of it. Even when he glanced around the shack, he didn't put what he thought in the form of a question. He just said, "How long was Holly with you."

"You're doing the talking."

"Don't stall, Mike. This is serious."

Monty meant it just that way. The deputy sheriff suspected murder. The bruise on old Jake's head was not yet explained. In any case, the similarity to Ted's accident was too pat to ignore, as Monty pointed out.

"What's that got to do with me, Monty?"

"I think you know."

"Go on."

"Holly is Ted's wife."

"You think I tried to get him?"

"He nearly died," Monty said. "He may yet die."

"I didn't have anything to do with Ted's busted head —but I did fish him out of the water."

Monty looked right at Mike.

"How about Jake's busted head?"

"Monty, for God's sake."

"He's dead."

"Listen," Mike said. "I never even saw Jake last night."

"But," Monty said softly, "he's dead."

Mike lit another cigarette.

"Well," he said. "I sure as hell didn't kill him to get Holly. It wasn't necessary. After all," he finished sarcastically, "you've just told me she was here."

"That's right."

"Well?"

"With Jake gone," Monty said, "she and Ted will get everything he had. If Ted dies now, she'll get it all."

"So?"

"Have you asked her to marry you, by any chance?" "Yes," Mike admitted tightly. "I have."

"Now she'll be worth more than two hundred thousand dollars, if Ted dies." Monty paused. "Before, with Jake alive, she was just another dame."

"Why, you son of a bitch."

Monty ignored the insult. As far as he was concerned, Mike was under suspicion, and he said so. Monty was not satisfied with Ted's accident, either. From what he said, Mike realized he had talked to Carla. Apparently she had not come out and said she had seen Mike push Ted into the slough but Monty suspected that she had more to tell. On top of that Mike had a compound motive. A girl—and her money.

"Monty," Mike said, "you're crazy."

"I hope so." Monty turned on his heavy heel, started for the house and Holly.

The rest of the morning passed in confusion. Mike was warned not to leave Slat Landing and, while he serviced boats and kept the fuel dock in operation, men from the Sheriff's office went over every inch of the fuel dock. A carload of newspaper men came down from San Francisco. Mike was news. Pictures were taken. His fight career was rehashed. Hundreds of questions were asked. So it was not until afternoon that Mike got a chance to talk to Holly alone.

Even then it was for only a few minutes in the kitchen and, sitting at the table, barely touching her coffee, Holly looked drained of blood. Her blond hair was brushed back from her pale cheeks and tied in the usual thick ponytail. There was a faint trace of lipstick on the curve of her mouth. The high collar of her pale-blue dress buttoned up to her throat. But her tan seemed to have grayed. Her eyes were dulled.

"Mike."

"Yes, Holly."

"Jake is gone."

"Well?"

She looked up at him. Mike stared into her dulled eyes. For a moment, the noises from outside faded—the footsteps, voices, sounds of cars coming and going. In the sink the leaky faucet dripped in measured cadence. At the window, in the heat of the hot sun, a fly buzzed clumsily and suddenly, time shifting, Mike remembered old Jake and Ted playing cribbage. That night could have been a million years ago. Now, one was dead, the other maybe dying. Had she done it? God, she had wanted the old man dead. Hadn't they talked about it? Sure they had. Smoke came soothingly in his throat and nostrils.

He said stupidly, "Did you kill Jake?"

"Mike," she said, "did you?"

"I've got to know."

"Mike, you're a fool. What goes on in your head?"

"We wanted him dead."

"Please."

"Damn it, we talked about it. I'd hate to count the times we looked at that float and thought how easy it would be to get rid of him. You wanted a shot at his money. That was all that mattered to you. You said so."

"Mike," she pleaded, "don't. You're twisting the knife in me." A sob choked her, but he noticed no tears. "I'm not pretending. I wanted everything. But it was all talk."

"Talk, yes. And thinking. Maybe planning, even scheming."

She blinked. Her eyes seemed to clear a little.

"You don't understand, Mike. I'd learned to like old Jake. I wouldn't have hurt him for the world. Last night, after you left, we talked. It was as if I really was his daughter. He loved me. My own father never loved me." She took a deep breath. "We went to bed. I fell asleep and didn't wake up until a few minutes after midnight. You see, I'd set the alarm so I could keep my date with you. After I shut off the clock there wasn't a sound in the house. When I went down to you, I thought Jake was sleeping in his bed." Her voice thinned. "Mike, believe me, I couldn't have made love if—" She let the sentence dwindle into silence.

Mike wanted to believe. The beat of her name hammered on the rim of his mind: Holly, Holly. Tears sparkled at last on her lashes but her eyes, looking into his, never wavered. Oh, God, I love her. Cigarette smoke curled, lifting, weaving. His fingers shook. Hell, there was no law against the old man having an accident. Let Monty and the sheriff root all they liked. He had not killed the old man. Holly said she had not, either. She deserved faith. After all, she was still a kid. Kids all talked big.

"Holly," he said, "swear."

"Swear what?"

"That you're telling me the truth."

She blinked. "Mike, I swear it."

"All right," he said. He looked away from her and studied his cigarette. "Holly, how do you think it happened?"

She could not imagine. The old man had behaved as usual; everything had been the same. Before going to bed, he had taken one of his sleeping pills. As usual, he had gone right to sleep. She had heard him up and down half a dozen times. Once he had gone out to putter around the kitchen. After that, she had fallen asleep herself.

"You didn't wake until after midnight?"

"That's right, Mike. I set the alarm a little carelessly."

"You didn't hear anything?"

"No."

She took a deep breath and talked slowly. In her opinion, Jake must have wandered to the fuel dock for some reason or other. Maybe he had simply been restless but had not wanted to take another pill. At any rate, in the dark, Jake must have broken through the railing and plunged into the water.

Holly bowed her head. "He couldn't swim, Mike."

"I know. You told me."

"I wish I could bring him back."

"How about the money? It's all yours now. Yours and Ted's. You're a rich girl."

She lifted her head. "I don't want to talk about it."

"You always did before."

"Don't rub it in, Mike. Even if I deserve it, don't say it." Her voice shook. "I know it's too late for regrets but I'm sorry. I just hope that wherever Jake is now, he knows I want to be forgiven. This isn't what I wanted to have happen." She stopped, wiping her cheeks with the tips of her fingers. "Believe me, Mike."

"Does that matter? Whether I believe you or not?"

"More than anything. You're all I have."

He put out his cigarette. "Maybe," he said finally, "later on you won't feel that way."

"Why won't I?"

"For one thing," Mike said, "Monte and the sheriff have an idea that I'm responsible for Jake's death." He grinned. "For that matter, they have an idea they can pin Ted's fall on me, too. Funny?"

"Insane!"

"We know, but they don't."

Holly reached over the table and touched Mike's hand. "I'm not afraid," she said.

"You mean you trust me? You don't think I'd do what you thought of doing?"

But ironies were lost on her. "I love you, Mike," she said.

"Isn't that the same thing?"

Holly shook her head. "No, Mike, I don't think so. Trust has something to do with all kinds of hedges and covering your bets and making calculations. Everything you know and have seen and heard has to be taken into account. But love just is. I love you, and that hasn't got anything to do with anything else. It's just there, all by itself. No matter what else changed, that would always be the same. So it isn't like a trust. It isn't something I can lose or gain, according to various happenings." "Never?"

"Never, Mike."

He waited. Her eyes stared into his.

Anything.

I'll give you anything.

Just ask me.

The circle turned, repeating. He remembered Holly. Holly, Holly… And then, just before Monte and the sheriff and the newspaper men came barging back up into the kitchen, she put it into words for him one more time.

"I love you, Mike."

"I know," he said slowly. "I won't ever forget. Not ever."

He believed himself, too.

CHAPTER SIXTEEN

BY FRIDAY, Mike had been around the track so many times he knew all the turns. Either Monty or the sheriff, or both of them together, would start questions circling.

"Did you kill Jake?"

"No."

"Don't lie, Mike."

"I'm not lying."

"Jake didn't just drown."

"You said that."

"We're saying it again. Maybe Jake got the bruise on his head by falling. But a man who has spent his life on this fuel dock doesn't just go and fall into deep water in the middle of the night. And if he did, he'd know how to get back. There's a ladder ten feet away. No, Mike. Somebody shoved him through that railing—when he was unconscious or nearly so."

"You're not convincing me."

"Mike, aren't you in love with Holly?"

"I don't deny it. I am."

"She could become a wealthy girl. Not exactly rich, but quite well off."

"Agreed."

"All right, if you didn't do it, who did?"

"How the hell would I know?"

"Don't yell, Mike. You're not a big-time fighter now. You're just another guy pumping gas on a dirty fuel dock. Don't let all those newspaper characters give you the big head. Maybe, like we've heard, you're going to make a splash spilling what you know about fight fixes. But right now, right here, you're just a small-time punk. We've got you all measured for something pretty rotten."

"God damn it, you're wrong."

"It wasn't you, Mike?"

"Hell, no."

"Was it Holly?"

"You know it couldn't be."

"No, Mike. We don't know. We're just asking. Did you hear we found a little circle of cigarette butts up there in the weeds on the bank?"

"No."

"Does it mean anything to you?"

"No."

"We've got a hunch someone spent a lot of time there."

"So?"

"Somebody was watching the fuel dock, Mike. We have an idea that somewhere, when we find him, we have a witness to what happened to Jake."

"Is that supposed to scare me?"

"Does it?"

"No."

Mike always said the word stubbornly, keeping his answers short, but he never could guess what either the sheriff or Monty were thinking. They just kept plugging away, asking, checking, and Holly caught her share of questions, too.

"I'm worried," she told Mike. "They never leave me alone. Only, I can't help, Mike. I thought Jake was in his bed asleep. Remember? I told you."

"That's right."

She trembled. "I said a lot of crazy things, Mike. I really thought I wanted the money more than anything else. But Jake was good to me."

"You were good to him."

"He loved me, Mike."

"I know that."

"I wish they would let us forget, Mike. I wish everybody would go away and let us be happy." She paused, hugging her arms around his neck, lifting against him, touching her lips to his mouth.

"I love you, Holly. Jake loved you, but I love you differently."

"I should hope sol" She gave her first smile since Jake's death. "Everything will be all right, won't it, Mike? We didn't do anything to harm Jake. I didn't and I know you didn't. They won't take you away from me?"

"They have no reason to, Holly.

"Then we don't have to worry?"

"No, Holly. We'll be all right."

Mike had the far-out feeling of walking on those words. Once, as a kid, he hitched his way to the Yosemite to see snow. He could remember walking that white crust and trying not to let it break under him, and it had a sameness to threading those endless words, those torturing considerations. They don't send an innocent man to the gas chamber. Or do they? The thought needled, jabbed, rubbed him raw in the sleepless night, nagged through the days, working, talking fish, fueling, pumping gas, adding figures, pretending right always made might when he knew better.

He had not killed Jake but, if the sheriff and Monty were not wrong, someone had. Why were they so sure? Accidents happened. There were always a half-dozen possible explanations for everything. A man like Jake, panicked in the water, could do a lot of nonsensical things. An old man, falling in, could have forgotten about the ladder from the water to the dock. Anyway, Jake could not swim.

Monty was out of his mind. The sheriff was, too. But they went right on digging and it was no secret that they kept everyone under observation. That included Fat Joe and Carla. From Monty, Mike knew they were both being questioned but up until late Saturday night, when Carla telephoned, Mike stayed away from the hotel.

Even then, slipping into his jacket, leaving the fuel dock to walk swiftly through the darkness, he could not figure out whether Carla were really in trouble and needed him or if she had been putting on an act. Over the telephone she had not given him a chance to ask questions.

"Mike," she had whispered. "I need help. Help me, Mike."

"What's wrong, Carla?"

"I'm hurt."

"Hurt!"

"Fat Joe did it. Mike, hurry. Help me. I can't ask anyone else."

That was all. That, and the soft catch of her breath sobbing, the click of the connection breaking. Trying to call back, Mike had not been able to get an answer but he knew one thing for sure. He did not want her telling any phony stories about seeing him shove Ted into the slough. Mike had enough troubles with Monty and the sheriff already. The thought echoed in the crunch of his footsteps. The wide porch creaked. Inside, behind the desk, the night clerk was filing mail. When Mike passed, the clerk looked around only long enough to say the elevator wasn't working.

Upstairs, a radio blared behind the door marked twenty-one. Two women were talking, both at the same time. Somewhere in the rear of the building a door slammed. Outside, a motorcycle blasted past. Mike stopped at Carla's room. He waited a moment, listening, and then he rapped.

"Carla?"

He rapped softly again and then tried the knob. The door was not locked. Hinges made a low squeaking. He stepped inside. But for a thin streak of light slanting in through the window drapes, the room was dark. In that faint reflection Mike saw Carla sprawled on the bed. Black lace panties hugged her hips but except for that she was naked. Shadows moved with the curving mounds of her breasts. The black tangle of her hair flared against the white pillow. She stirred.

"Mike?"

"That's right. Me."

He closed the door behind himself. At the bed, he leaned over. She turned her head to look up at him. Her lashes fluttered.

"Mike," she whispered.

He touched the bruise on her cheek. A trace of blood smeared her mouth. She moaned.

"He hit me."

Mike moved his hands over her. She winced with the touch of his fingers on her breast.

"Is it bad, Carla?"

She waited, breathing deeply.

"I'll live," she said at last. Her mouth trembled but suddenly, with tears pooling, wetting her cheeks, she forced a bitter smile. "I've been hurt worse."

"Take it easy. You can tell me later."

"No. I want to talk. Look at me. I'm not an old woman and I never wanted to hurt anybody. And look at me. Maybe living is like getting a road map. This is you, that damned line right there. There are all the things you'll see, the places you'll go. It must be like that. I never planned to be what I am. I never planned to wind up this way."

"Why did Joe do it?"

She ignored the question.

"I'm a whore. It has an ugly sound, doesn't it?" You can't make that word pretty. It's all kinds of dirty little rooms and rumpled beds. It's dirty money crumpled under a pillow and fat mouths and hands and taking something beautiful and selling it for so much a night."

"Carla."

Mike lit a cigarette and gave it to her. He lit one for himself. The flickering flame glowed on the richness of her figure.

Darkness tipped her breasts. She inhaled deeply. He pocketed his lighter. Smoke lifted. She moved her hand. The red glow of her cigarette burned a hot circle in the dim shadows.

"Ugly," she whispered. "That's the story of my life. You ought to know, Mike. You were part of it. Remember all the big nights? New York, Detroit, Chicago, New Orleans, Vegas, Los Angeles. Oh, God, you really believed. Mike Shannon, the fisher boy with fists of gold. All the time Joe made sure you didn't get beaten." Carla's mouth twisted. "How dumb can you get? We all used to pull a big laugh out of it. After a fight, after you were asleep, we would sit around and tell stories. Sure, good old Carla, she'll do anything. Lie about love or marriage. Be nice to Fat Joe. Why not? After all, you can't wear out a whore." She stopped suddenly. Then, her voice breaking, she whispered, "I always wanted to stop. I did, Mike. I had a dream about a house of my own and shopping at the supermarket. Sounds awful, doesn't it?"

"No."

"Well, it is. Awful. And impossible. I know it. Even so I didn't want to come up here for Fat Joe. I didn't care about his plans. I really didn't want to see you again. I knew it would be no use. Why should you trust me? If you had slapped me around, I would only have gotten what I deserved. But Joe wanted to be sure you'd keep your mouth shut."

"We've already talked that over," he reminded her.

"Yes."

"I said I wouldn't sound off. I said I wouldn't spill anything."

"Yes."

"Didn't you tell Fat Joe?"

"Yes."

Mike smoked angrily.

"Well," he said at last, "wasn't that enough?"

"Nothing is enough for Joe."

"I know," Mike said harshly. "Believing would come hard to that fat bastard."

Carla moved painfully. Mike went to the bathroom and brought back a damp wash cloth. He wiped her face gently. All the time, Carla kept looking right up at him and then finally, when he covered her with the spread, she went back to talking about Fat Joe. Her voice shook.

"I'm not a slave, Mike."

"No."

"But that's what I am to him. Nothing. Nobody. Just do as you're told. Go to bed with whoever I want you to."

"Tell him to go to hell."

She shook her head.

"It's not that simple. Look at me."

"I'm looking."

"He hit me, Mike."

"But you got him what he was after. I promised to keep my mouth shut."

"I told him."

"Then it wasn't that?"

"No."

Carla turned her cheek against the pillow. Mike waited. In the hall, footsteps passed the door. Outside, under the window, there was the patter of running feet. A kid started yelling. As the sounds faded, Mike went back to asking questions. At first, Carla made no sense. She talked about the story she had threatened to tell, the one about seeing him with Ted Adam the night Ted fell. Apparently Joe had hinted at it to Monty but then when Joe knew Mike didn't intend to talk to the reporters. Joe wanted the rumor stopped.

"Okay," Mike said. "That should be easy. After all, you couldn't have seen me that night. When Ted almost drowned, I was in the shack asleep."

Carla did not seem to be listening.

"I want to start being right, Mike," she said. "Not for you. I know there can't be anything between us, but I want to be right for myself."

"Go on."

"I didn't see you with Ted that night, Mike—but I didn't make up the story either. If you pull back the drape you'll be able to make out the path around the back of the cannery. You can see it all the way from here."

"Yes, Carla?"

"I was looking out that night, Mike."

He got up from the edge of the bed. At the window, he pushed aside the drape. For a moment he stood motionless. Beyond the road, he could follow the line of the path. Behind the cannery, where the bank was steep, the path twisted above the water. Light glittered where Ted had been found half-drowned. Mike let the drape fall back into place. He walked to the bed and sat down on the edge.

"You saw Ted?"

"Yes," Carla said.

"Somebody else?"

"Yes."

Mike waited and then Carla made a helpless gesture with her hand.

"I've heard the talk, Mike. It might be that you're in for a bad time. I could stop that, maybe. Anyway, I wanted to go to the sheriff with my story. I know the kind of damage that publicity could do to me but I'm tired of running, Mike. I want to be somebody. If I got free of Fat Joe, whatever happened to me wouldn't matter. No, don't touch me, Mike. I've got to say this right. I love you but, even if I didn't, even if it were somebody else, I'd want to go to the sheriff." Her voice broke. "That was what I tried to tell Joe. I want to start from here. I want to stop running, stop being afraid... But I don't have any rights with him. He owns me. When he says talk, I talk. When he says shut up, I shut up."

"Is that how he came to beat you?"

"Yes."

"He didn't want you to tell what you had seen?"

"No."

"Why, Carla?"

"Oh, God," she said. "You know him. Now that he's decided you aren't going to make any scandal talking about him, he doesn't want me involved in trouble. It might lead to him, he figures."

"Is he coming back?"

"Yes," she whispered. "This was what he called a sample. He said he was sure that after I had time to think it over, I wouldn't do anything foolish."

"Have you thought it over?"

"Yes, Mike." She took a deep breath. "I'm not brave." She rolled puffy eyes at him. "But I intend to talk to the sheriff."

"It might mean digging up your past."

"I know."

"But you're willing to take the chance for me?"

"Yes," Carla whispered. Her voice trembled. "For you, and for me. I owe you something."

"Not your life."

"Yes," she said simply. "If you need it, Mike, even my life."

A moment passed.

"All right," he said finally. "Who did you see that night?"

Carla stared up at him.

"I know," she said slowly, "that someone else was on the path when Ted was there."

Someone had slipped into the room, but neither of them knew it. Mike did not even hear the door click. Maybe, with all the ugliness of the past still bitter and alive in him, he should have sensed the heaviness behind him; but Mike just kept staring down at Carla. Fat Joe had come in, but she was no more aware of it than Mike, and her lips moved.

"Yes," she said again. "Someone was there."

She studied Mike. He took a deep breath. Memory turned. Monty had said that Ted had been struck on the head. Mike rubbed his mouth. His tongue felt dry and thick. He was about to speak, but he saw Carla lift her head, stare over his shoulder, her eyes wide.

"Joe," she whispered.

The hair prickled on the back of Mike's neck. He moved carefully, turning, keeping his hand still. A small emptiness twisted in the pit of his stomach. By the door, a hand moved. The light switch snapped. In the bright glare, the room cut sharp shadows. The mirror over the dresser reflected hardness. A perfume bottle glittered and, with the door closed behind him, Joe squeezed a stubby automatic in his pudgy hand. On one finger, an outsized diamond flashed.

Fat Joe.

Big? Yes, he was big. Gross? Sure, that was the word. Not just fat or overstuffed but gross. Thick, wadded flesh, eyes holed in suet, lips puffed like a pig's snout. He had a way of breathing noisily through mouth and nose at the same time, swallowing air. A gray suit stretched over his beefy shoulders and columns of legs. One miserable wisp of black hair was combed wet over his bald head.

The gun moved.

"Get up, Mike," growled Fat Joe.

Mike stood up. The blubber, the puffiness, were all on the outside; underneath them, Joe was stone. He had no mercy. It wasn't something you thought about or decided. You knew it. Everything was the same to Joe: eating, going to bed with girls, killing, cheating, or pulling the trigger of a gun. Whatever it was, he always had everything figured. When minds had been passed out, he'd been an adding machine; a cold, hard calculator that had no feelings, no sensibilities.

Mike blinked. Light glinted steel. The diamond sparkled and Joe shifted his eyes a little, looking at Carla.

"Did you telephone Mike?"

"Yes."

"I told you not to talk to anybody."

"You told me."

"But you called Mike?"

"Yes," Carla said.

"Get up, Carla."

Mike shifted his weight.

"Joe."

"You got something to say, Mike?"

"Don't touch her again."

Joe's colorless eyes flicked from Carla to Mike and then back to Carla again. He sniffed, opening his mouth, swallowing air. Mike could practically hear the adding machine clicking. For once, Joe had got himself trapped. Like a dog burying too many bones, he had not been able to keep everything hidden at once. While he had been pushing dirt over what Mike might reveal about the gambling behind his career, Ted had got himself hospitalized. That must have seemed like a break to Joe at first. But now, instead of having Carla threatening to make trouble for Mike, Joe had Carla threatening to tell the truth. That would surely bring up her past and once that was in the open, Joe could hardly keep himself clean. At the same time, he could not risk firing a shot here in the hotel. The law was the last thing in the world he needed in his hair. That thought was as tangible to Mike as if Fat Joe had put it into words. So there was not going to be any shooting. There was not going to be any more hammering on Carla. If she had not scared enough to see things Joe's way, there was nothing the fat man could do but pretend it did not matter. Wait for the dust to settle. There was always another day, another twist, another chance.

Joe shrugged. The gun lowered.

"Believe me, Mike," he said smoothly. "Maybe I used extreme measures with Carla but I did it for her own good."

Mike said, "I've heard almost everything out of you, Fat Boy—but working a woman over for her own good? That's news."

"I was trying to keep her from walking into a noose."

"That bad?"

"It could be."

"Taking your advice would be better?"

"Much better. For her. For me. For you, even."

Mike laughed.

"No, Joe. Not for me. Most likely I could clear myself of any charge that I conked Ted or old Jake—because I didn't. But I've been through your mill. I had it good and I had it bad. I beat some men I shouldn't have beaten and I got whipped by a man who knew his business, by a man out of my class. But when it was all over, Joe, I had nothing. Remember how funny that was? God, did you laugh. You said with expenses and training and taxes, I should have known, but I was just a dumb fisherman. You proved then that nothing about you could ever be good for me."

"It's possible," Joe said, "there might be some adjustment of those conditions."

Mike sent a glance at Carla. "Do you think I ought to trust Joe?"

"No."

"Oh?"

"Mike I'd give you my promise. Just you don't talk— and don't let Carla talk."

"Fatso, your word doesn't seem to hold much water around here." He waited. Joe backed toward the door, but Mike shook his head. "Not yet," he said. "I'm interested in that adjustment."

"It would take time."

"How much time?"

"Mike," Joe said, "don't do anything foolish."

"Scared?"

Joe rapped out, "I'm never scared."

"I think you are."

Mike had whispered the words. The room narrowed to Joe. Just fat Joe. Nothing else. Not even Carla moving, slipping into her robe. Mike squeezed his fists. He heard his own voice, bitter, soft.

So Joe had come down to insure silence, had he? God, that was a laugh. What do I know—a dumb fisherman? A sucker, a big believer, with my eyes blinded by glitter. My God, all the reporters in the world could fire questions at me for a month and I wouldn't have a single fact to hurt you. Does that make sense? Too bad you couldn't have realized that, Joe. Only from where you operate, it's pretty hard to see straight.

Those were the words that came raggedly out of his mouth. Mike swore. He wanted to stop talking. Hell, Joe didn't care what he had to say. But Mike kept on, compulsively spouting his bitterness. No, don't wave that damned gun at me. Had he said that? Of course he had. Joe wasn't going to do any shooting. Pulling the trigger wouldn't solve any problems. Joe was too smart to do anything silly. This time, you fat bastard, I've got you where I want you. Nobody around to slug me from behind with a gun butt, either.

"Easy," Joe said. "Easy Mike. I warn you."

"Go to hell."

"Don't hit me, Mike."

"Why not? Adding machines don't shoot bullets."

Mike set his shoulders. The quickness came back, tingling his arms. He took a deep breath. Joe hefted the gun. He would not shoot. But he would slug. Sure. He would fight back. Mike turned a little, instinctively moving like a boxer. Joe did not have a chance.

Feinting, slipping to avoid the clumsy swing Joe made with the gun, Mike jabbed the fat face. He shifted and drove his right into Joe's huge paunch. Mike was not just pounding the breath out of Joe; Mike was destroying. The squish of lardy flesh was the whole damned way of life, the big dreams collapsing like a pricked balloon. Well, to hell with it. Smash every damned thing. He hit viciously. Joe sagged in the corner. The wet smack of his face blobbed. Mike heard the gun clatter to the floor. Smash. Don't let this be lost too. He heard the hard suck of his own breath. The memory of what he and Carla had said to each other flashed into his head. To hell with that, too. Old Jake was dead. Nobody was going to bring him back. Mike slashed mercilessly. They had taken everything else but nobody was going to take Holly. She was the answer, the whole meaning. Let somebody else worry about truth. Nobody had worried when he had hit the skids. Mike grunted. Smash. Blood smeared his fists and then dimly, her hands beating, her voice begging, Carla got through to him.

"Mike—stop. Stop. You're killing him!"

Mike blinked his eyes. The room cleared. Joe puffed painfully, struggling to stay on his feet. To keep him from falling, Mike had wedged him into the corner. One eye was closed. Blood trickled out of the corner of his mouth.

"You son of a bitch," the pig snout said.

Mike stared. He felt sick. It would be easier if Joe got down and crawled but he wasn't going to do that. Fat, ugly, rotten and no good, but standing. It didn't make sense. But what did? Mike opened his hands. His fingers were sticky.

"You son of a bitch," Joe snarled, pig lips bloody. He looked like a butchered carcass.

Carla put her hands on Mike's chest.

"No more."

"Don't worry," Mike said softly. "The adjustment has been made." He stared at Fat Joe. "Pick up your gun. Get out. Don't come back."

"Now you feel big? You beat me, punk. But you didn't scare me."

"Yeah," Mike said. "That makes you almost as good as Carla."

At last alone with Carla again, his hands and arms wet from washing, the taste of Carla's whiskey hot in his stomach, Mike remembered the way Fat Joe had walked out. No more remarks. No cleaning himself up. Nothing. Just the door closing, the heavy footsteps fading down the length of the hall.

"I wanted to squash him, Carla."

"I know, Mike."

"But it was no good."

"I could have told you," she whispered.

"Why, Carla?"

She shook her head.

"I figured he'd turn yellow."

"Life isn't a movie."

"You mean the good guy doesn't always win?"

"Something like that, Mike."

Mike offered her a cigarette. She took it, but did not smoke. He lit one for himself. Then, going on, talking softly about Fat Joe, Mike told Carla he had probably made things worse.

"No," she said. "He won't be back."

"You're guessing. Hoping."

"I know Fat Joe."

She walked to the window.

"I know him," she said. "In a lot of ways, Joe and I are alike. You can't get dirty without learning what it is to walk in the gutter. You expect hard knocks but you soon learn to keep grudges out of business. Joe took his beating. Getting back at us would likely make a mess out of his political plans. You told him you can't hurt him. He's sure I have enough sense enough to keep my mouth shut about him, rather than risk beatings, persecution, maybe a murder trial. As long as things stay like that, he won't bother us again. You steal on your side of the patch and I'll steal on mine. That's the way Joe thinks." She stopped and tugged the edge of the drape back. Then, without turning, she said, "You weren't just fighting Joe. Mike, a man doesn't hit to smash like you did without a good reason. You're the one who's afraid—aren't you?"

"Afraid?"

"Yes, Mike."

"Why would I be afraid?"

"I think you know, Mike."

She paused. He walked to stand behind her. Light shimmered blackly in her dark hair. Her robe fell in soft folds to the floor. On the drape, her fingers trembled. Lifting from the Blue Gull, the bass beat of the juke box throbbed with hillbilly music. On the road, car lights glared in the night. Reflections glittered in the harbor. Red and green running lights moved down the channel. A diesel muttered softly. Where the path passed behind the cannery, shadows deepened.

"All right, Carla. You think I know what?"

She didn't turn.

"Don't make it hard."

"I'm waiting, Carla."

He bit down on the words and then inhaled. The tip of his cigarette burned hot. Tobacco smoke stung his lungs. The emptiness came back, the big hole of nothingness, the way he had felt before battering Joe. Memory lifted, revealing the hard edge of what Carla had been saying. He took another deep drag at his cigarette.

"Carla," he said impatiently, "you were going to tell who you saw on that path with Ted."

"All right," she whispered. "I know this will be hard to say but, at least, Mike I owe you the truth. What you do with it is up to you." She paused.

"Go on, Carla."

"Mike," she said softly, "I saw a man behind Ted. A big man. It could have been you, Mike."

He let time pass. A moment. A minute. Several minutes. He lit another cigarette. He stared through the window.

"It was too far," Mike said, "to make out the face."

"Yes."

"You don't know it was me, Carla. You don't even know it was Ted."

"Have it your way." She hesitated. "Mike, if you want to do it to me now, you can. Not because you kept fat Joe off me. Because I love you. Don't you know I love you?"

Mike clenched his fists, felt the tingle of his barked knuckles.

"Are you telling me that if you can have me, you won't tell Monty what you saw?"

She turned and looked at him. She seemed about to cry, but unexpectedly the red lips stiffened.

"Get out of here," she said. "Mike—you get out of here."

CHAPTER SEVENTEEN

SATURDAY, AND in the Blue Gull, easing through the crowd, Mike reached a stool at the end of the bar. He ordered a double whiskey and lit a cigarette. Mig waved. Hank served the drink. A drunk started arguing with his wife. They yapped back and forth. The juke box pounded. Smoke hazed bluishly. Mike drained his drink and ordered again. A slim, young brunette stopped to stare drunkenly at him.

"You Mike Shannon?"

"That's right."

"How would you like something nice?"

"What's nice?"

"Guess."

"Look, honey," Mike said wearily. "It's nearly midnight. Why don't you go home and rest up?"

"Aren't you the fighter?"

"I did some fighting."

"I'd like a guy like you." She blinked and made an exaggerated movement with her hips. "We could make beautiful music."

"No, thanks."

Her expression changed.

"Why, you dirty son of a bitch."

Mig edged through the crowd.

"All right, sister," she said to the brunette. "Take what you've got and trot it back to daddy."

"I want something new."

"That's fine," Mig said. "Write us a letter."

"Us?"

"Yes," Mig said. "Us."

"It's like that?"

"Yes," Mig said.

The brunette wobbled.

"I can find somebody else."

"Sure." Mig smiled. "You keep trying."

The brunette staggered, wandered back down the bar. Mike thanked Mig.

He hung around until closing time, and they left together. A dark, salt mist drifted across the crests of the barren sand dunes. Dotted in the night, a few lights glowed yellow. There was a brawl going on in the parking lot. A woman squealed and then cursed shrilly. The red light of the patrol car blinked. Loose gravel crunched.

Mig held on to Mike's arm. They turned to go down the alley. The noise from the parking lot faded, muting in with the steady sound of the surf breaking on the sea side of the landing. In the channel, a big purse-seiner, one of the few remaining sardine boats, chugged toward the mooring wharves. Overhead, in the blackness, sea gulls mewed unseen, calling back and forth. Far off, beyond the highway, a freight train rumbled toward Monterey.

"Mike?"

"Yes, Mig. Hell, you don't have to sound so worried."

"Oh, I am worried. Have you seen Herb?"

"No. I wouldn't know him if I did see him."

"He's still around." She paused. "I told you he has a gun."

"Sure," Mike said. "I remember."

"He gets crazy, Mike."

"We all do, Mig."

Mig looked up.

"Has something bad happened?"

Mike shook his head. No, nothing bad had happened. He got out his cigarettes. He lit one for her and one for himself. The movement of her hip brushed it against him and she would not let him change the subject. "What happened?"

"Nothing."

"Don't lie, Mike. I can tell."

"Tell what?"

"Something has happened."

He let her do the talking. The sound of her voice slanted off the surface of his mind. He smelled night, garbage, salt mist, the rot of wetted wood and the fish and the ice-damp. A cat darted through the shadows. I ought to go home, to the shack, he thought. His head ached. Love? Everybody searched for love. It was the whole meaning of everything. I love Holly. Oh, my God, I've got to have her. What else is there? To hell with right and wrong. Let somebody else figure out bad and good and black and white.

"Mike?"

"Sorry, Mig. I wasn't listening."

She told him it didn't matter and then, at her place, she asked him in. They had coffee in the kitchen. Light glared on Mig's platinum hair. Platinum, this week. Lipstick stained the rim of her cup. They smoked another cigarette and finally, still prying, Mig asked if he had been at the hotel seeing Carla. She waited but Mike let the subject die. Instead of making an effort to pick it up, Mig suddenly veered back to Herb and then abruptly she asked Mike about Holly.

"Do you love her?"

"Holly?"

Mig mimicked, "Holly? Oh, for God's sake, Mike. Don't be so cautious." She got up from the table. He followed to her bedroom. She snapped on the small lamp. When he stopped inside the doorway, she told him to come on in. "You don't have to make love to me."

"That wasn't what I was thinking."

"Wasn't it?"

She smiled sadly and then, her back to him, she wriggled out of her black sweater. A moment later, opening the zipper, she stepped out of the Capri pants. Nylon shimmered, hiding nothing. Her hips moved. Legs flashed. At her closet she took out a negligee. Before slipping into it, she undid her bra. Turning, tying the belt around her slim waist, she walked back to the bed.

"We were talking about Herb."

"And Holly."

"Yes," Mig said. "And Holly."

"Go on, Mig."

"Curious?"

"Yes," Mike said. "I am."

"Maybe Herb was right."

"About what, Mig?"

"He said you loved Holly."

Mike waited and Mig put her arms behind herself, bracing her hands on the bed. Platinum hair framed her elfin face. Lipstick heightened the curve of her mouth, but even with the loose folds of her negligee breathing up with the lift of her firm young breasts, she was remote. It was as if she had drawn into herself and all the suggestive stripping was no longer a promise or a hope. Whatever she had meant to do she no longer intended and the mistiness in her eyes, the throb of her pulse beating in the hollow of her throat, gave her the aspect of a shy and puzzled child.

"Mike?"

"Yes, Mig."

"Remember being here with me?"

Hurt turned ragged in her voice. She swallowed, her lips trembling. Then as she asked the question again, Mike tried to keep from answering.

"Mig," he said. "We were talking about Herb."

"I know." She moved, turning a little, drawing up her legs to sit on the bed with her ankles crossed. She drew the folds of her negligee together, hugging her arms around her knees. She looked young, small, very lonely. The platinum shimmer in her hair was suddenly pathetic, like a frightened child's attempt at defiance. "I know," she said again. "But I don't want to talk about Herb or Holly, any more. I want to talk about us."

"Mig—"

She looked up.

"No, Mike. Don't stop me. I want to remember. I guess a man doesn't keep every small thing but I'm not like a man. We were right here. I was some drunk but not too much. I felt like silk, like naked satin." She blinked her eyes and forced a smile. "That sounds silly, doesn't it, Mike?"

"No, Mig."

"Yes," she whispered. "It does. Most things get silly. It's like all the treasures you save when you're a kid. When you go through them, it's hard to remember why they were so important." She closed her eyes. "Like sleek silk," she murmured. "Oh, God, I wanted you so much. All my life, all through school, all the time you were away, I thought about how it would be to belong to you." She bent her head so all he could see was the top of her head and the light platinum hair. "Did you know, Mike?"

"Know?"

She looked up.

"Still cautious? Does it make you nervous to have me telling you how I felt? Well, don't mind, Mike. Sometimes words are like tears. If you let them come, you feel better. But then men don't cry. Oh, hell, I'm getting mixed up. Do all your women get mixed up, Mike? No," she went on quickly, "don't answer that." Her lashes fluttered. She went back to the way she had felt like satin. "That was for you, Mike. I wanted to hold everything, to be hurt, to be taken. Now it's gone. Isn't that silly? I've got my memory."

"Stop it, Mig."

She took a deep breath.

"All right, Mike." She paused. "Of course, you never did love me, did you? Not even a little bit. You didn't even know I was alive."

He stared at her.

"Not really," he said.

She closed her eyes.

"Why don't things come out even, Mike?"

"I don't know."

She opened her eyes. A smile quivered.

"You'd think if I loved you, you would love me or if Herb loved me, I would love him."

"Life is never perfect, Mig."

"Listen to Mike. The working girl's philosopher." She looked away from him. "Poor Herb. All the time the two of us were married, I guess he felt like I'm feeling. Do you think it's as tough on a man as it is on a woman?" She went on quickly without waiting for an answer. "It's hard to figure. You don't know what I feel. I don't know what you feel. All we have are words. Mostly they only scratch the surface. Even trying, I can't tell you how it feels to not be wanted. There aren't any words." She paused. "Oh, God, Mike, I'm sorry. I didn't mean to go to pieces on you." She let go of her knees and, twisting to get up, she said, "I just wanted to tell you that there's something Herb thinks he knows about you and Holly."

"Did he say what?"

"No."

Mig stood beside the bed, stood facing Mike.

"But whatever it is," she went on, "I had the feeling he was waiting to talk to you." She frowned. "Remember, Mike. Herb has a gun."

"I'll remember."

They walked back to the kitchen. Light glared harshly. Outside, where the road passed the head of the alley, a horn blared. The reflection of light rippled across the window shade but the quiet afterwards was the empty stillness of early morning. Coffee cups glinted on the table. The floor creaked softly under Mike's weight. Aloud, Mig recalled the brunette. They both laughed and then Mike took another step toward the door.

"It's late, Mig."

"I don't care."

"You'd better get some sleep."

"I won't sleep, Mike. I've got a lot to think about."

Mike forced himself to go to the door, open it.

"Mike?"

"Yes."

He stopped, standing with his hand on the knob. The metal felt cool under his fingers. Mig faced him. Under the filmy negligee, the tips of her breasts sought him, beckoned to him. Nylon traced the slender curves of her figure. He remembered the taut clinging, the supple yielding. He even felt the twist of her mouth shuddering against his. But it had not been too good; not the greatest. Maybe it could be better. All he had to do was reach out for her and he would have it all in his hands again. What the hell. Women were just women. He squeezed his eyes open and shut. Holly… Holly… The beat hammered across his mind. He wasn't going to reach for Mig. She had said it: nothing came out even. Oh, God, he thought. I've got to get out of here. Damn all of them. Damn Carla, and damn Mig, and damn—No. I've got to get back to Holly.

"Mike?"

He got hold of himself. "Mig, I've got to go,"

"You don't want to stay?"

"No."

"Can't you lie a little?"

"No," Mike said. "No more."

"It's done."

"Mig, there never was anything."

She did not move. She just stood with her hands clasped together.

"Yes," she said. "There was. Maybe it's like little boys dreaming about growing up to be cowboys or generals. Only it doesn't usually turn out. Well, it didn't turn out for me. I was going to be in love with you for all my life."

"I'm sorry, Mig."

She shook her head.

"I'm sorry too." She stopped. "Poor me," she whispered. "Poor Herb."

Mike opened the door.

"Good night, Mig."

"Good night," she said. "Good night and goodbye."

CHAPTER EIGHTEEN

MIKE TOOK a big breath of fresh air. Behind him the lock clicked. A moment later, the light went out. Below the steps, the alley was dark. The lid of a garbage can caught a thin slant of reflection from the wharves beyond the road. It glinted dully. Mike went down. Dirt scuffed. He walked toward the head of the alley and then, just at the corner, a shadow moved against the rear of a rotten crumbling old warehouse.

"Shannon?"

Mike stopped. He turned toward the voice.

"I'm Mike Shannon."

The shadow had a gun. Steel glistened in the sea mist, wetness moved with a leather jacket. Under damp, plastered hair, a thin face emerged. Big shoulders hunched. The free hand wiped back black hair.

"Do you know me?"

Mike waited. After what Mig had said, he had a good idea of who the other was. But with the gun aimed at his stomach, Mike made no sudden moves. The mouth grinned shakily.

"I'm Herb Sanky."

"Okay," Mike said.

"I've been looking for you."

"Yeah," Mike said. "I heard."

"I've been watching Mig's door."

Mike waited.

"Well," Herb said. "You were at her place."

Mike nodded.

"We had a cup of coffee."

The gun moved nervously.

"She loves you, doesn't she?"

Mike shrugged. "Why ask me? Ask her."

"By God," Herb snapped. "Don't get smart. You just answer when I ask you something. Don't think I ain't on top of this whole damn thing. Hell, man, you wrecked my marriage. I had everything nice but Mig was always cutting your pictures out of the papers. She kept them all pasted in a book. How would you like that? How would you like somebody you loved keeping pictures of a damn prize fighter?"

"It wasn't my fault."

"The night you got your licking, I was the happiest man in the whole United States. I watched it on TV. Every time you got up and got smacked again, it did me good. I hoped you'd get killed. But after that, things became even worse because Mig figured you'd be coming home. That was the real reason she went on over to Nevada and got her divorce. God damn you. You understand me?"

"Yes," Mike said.

"See this gun?"

"Yes," Mike said again.

"I could kill you. Honest to God, I thought about it plenty. All I got to do is squeeze this trigger. Just one little squeeze. That's all it would take. I meant to do it too. God damn it, I spent a long time waiting for you to come home the other night. Well, you didn't come but I saw things. I saw plenty. Now maybe I have you where I want you—without killing you."

Mike stared. The memory of Monty came back. They had found a place where someone had waited, smoking, watching the fuel dock. That must have been Herb. Mike took a deep breath. His throat tightened.

"All right," he managed to say at last. "Go on, Herb. What did you see?"

"I saw the old man and the girl."

"Jake and Holly?"

"Yes," Herb said. "That's right."

Mike waited. His hands were hot. Sweat wet his fingers. He breathed the stink of Slat Landing, the fish smell soaked into the very ground, the junk, rotting wood, tumble-down houses, crumbling cannery sheds and warehouses. His throat choked with the breath of dust from the power plant and the chemical refinery, the sludge stagnation of salt and mud and sedge grass. A big ugly fist smashed down in his brain. Holly. No, no ... Mike tensed. Nerves tingled. It was like the minutes before a fight, the last waiting. He saw shadows slashed sharp, a black and white clarity, broken boards over a shattered window in the warehouse, mist wet, light glistening on Herb's narrow face.

"I saw them," Herb said again.

"Go on."

"Her and the old man. It was dark. They were talking but I couldn't hear what they were saying. Then they went down them steps from the back porch." He paused, wetting his lips with the tip of his tongue. "I'd smoked five or six cigarettes so it must have been after eleven o'clock then."

Mike clenched his hands.

"Just tell me about Holly."

"She shoved the old man off the dock."

"No!"

The word came out hard, and with it, Mike hit, without thinking. To hell with the gun. To hell with everything. The big, bloaty bastard was lying. Mike jammed one hand against Herb. His fingers twisted in Herb's shirt front. Breath exploded. Mike belted Herb in the guts. The skinny face parted. A wet mouth gulped for air. But Herb held on to the gun. He wasn't going to use it but he still held it.

"Don't. You're choking me!"

Mike steadied. Hate tasted acid in his mouth. He kept his fingers clamped tight. Against the building, Herb struggled helplessly, moving his head from side to side but not letting go of the gun.

"Talk," growled Mike.

"I'm telling you the truth."

"Holly didn't kill the old man."

"She shoved him off the dock," Herb panted. "Christ," he said. "I was there. I saw her. The old man was leaning on the rail. The next thing, he was in the water."

"He fell."

Mike slapped the words into Herb's face. Heat burned up. The night flooded red. Rage hammered a big drum. Flesh crushed under his fingers. They took everything, he thought. I had the whole damned world and they took that. Now I've got Holly. Nobody will take her. Prayer, plea, smashed through the surface of his mind. No, no, no. God, please no. Breath gritted in his teeth.

Thin sounds that hissed out of Herb.

"She shoved him."

"Why didn't you stop her?"

"It happened too quick. It was like some kind of nightmare. First she was doing it and then he was gone. She stood there and brushed her dress and then just like nothing had happened she went back up to the house."

"No."

Herb wiggled helplessly.

"I saw her," he insisted.

"No."

"Yes, I saw."

Mike took a deep breath.

"All right," he said. "Why haven't you gone to the police?"

"I don't know."

"Listen you bastard," Mike snapped. "You know. You damned well know."

Herb bugged his eyes.

"I was going. I figured on telling Monty. But hell, once it was done, I couldn't help the old man. Besides, it was pretty nice knowing something big, and, what the hell do I owe Monty and the cops? They never did nothing for me. I thought about it some but then I got to remembering the talk I heard about you and her."

"Talk? What talk?"

"Damn it," Herb said, "you can't trot a girl down to the shack on the fuel dock without somebody knowing. Slat Landing ain't that kind of a place." Herb blinked his eyes, sucked breath with his mouth open. "Anyway," he finished. "I got to thinking that maybe, if you liked her, we could make a deal."

"Deal?"

The vein in Mike's forehead throbbed. Darkness held insanity. The narrow face talked. Light glinted. Across the slough, on the highway, a couple of freight trailers headed north to San Francisco. Exhaust roared in the night. Surf kept up a steady thudding, a sand-swishing; the thread of where they were and what they were saying held the minutes together. My God, Mike thought. I've got to get hold of myself. Then with that half whine, half bluster, Herb's voice hit again.

"Sure," he said. "I could send that girl to prison. Maybe the gas chamber. But I don't have to do it. I don't give a damn about her old Jake. All I care about is Mig."

"Mig?"

"Yes," Herb went on quickly. "God, she's got some crazy idea about you. If it wasn't for that, we could get back together. I love her. It don't matter to me about Holly but if you stay away from Mig forever, I'll keep my mouth shut." Herb made a thin, giggling sound. "As long as you know what I know, you've got that girl over a barrel. She'll have to do anything for you. Don't you see? It works out. I'll never say a word. And all you got to do is fix it so Mig knows you don't ever want to see her. I'll get Mig back."

Mike opened his hand. Herb wobbled, free but shaky. He rubbed his hand across his face. With the same motion, he pushed his lank hair back from his forehead. The pinched eyes glittered. Light punched back at Mike. He wanted to smash. His muscles ached to let go. He swallowed air. Jake was gone. Herb was right about that. The thought squeezed as Mike closed his fingers again. It was over. Done. Holly, Holly—he and Holly had talked about it, about Jake dead. I love her, Mike thought. The movement of her curved nakedly through his mind, the smooth legs, the swelling lift of her breasts, the softness across her stomach and the deep warmth waiting, the flood of heat flaring flame. To hell with thinking. It was done. Who was there to care? Right and wrong were words everybody used to suit themselves.

"Herb."

"Yes."

"Keep your mouth shut."

"You mean it's a deal?"

"You lunatic bastard," Mike whispered, "just be sure and keep your mouth shut."

"You'll stay away from Mig?"

"No."

Mike heard the sound of his voice, the hard shape of the word, short, chopped, and was astounded. Why not promise? Why not stay away from Mig? What did she matter? He remembered her eyes, the last goodbye, but Herb kept babbling, as though what he had to say made any difference. "I'll turn that girl in. I'll tell Monty." Herb brandished the gun, not knowing he held it.

Mike stared. Sickness churned in his stomach. Mig had said Herb was crazy, he was. Out of his mind. Otherwise, how could he think he could trade one woman for another? Mike looked into the burning eyes, full of fear and hatred. Mig was right. Crazy.

"No," Mike said again. "But if you breathe a word about what you told me, I'll find you, wherever you try to hide, and I'll beat you to death. You hear that? I'll beat you dead."

Mike turned.

What had come over him? He must be more insane, even, than Herb. Why hadn't he, Mike, been able to promise not to see Mig? Why did he, Mike, turn his back on a crazy man with a gun?

Mike walked off. If he took a shot between the shoulders he told himself, he would deserve it.

But no shot came.

CHAPTER NINETEEN

DARKNESS DEEPENED the road ruts. A light burned in the house. Holly's house, now. Ted's house. Not old Jake's. Mike stumbled. Where the ground was soft at the edge of the drive, sandy dirt crushed underfoot. Mike breathed wetness, the pale glimmer of fog. Below the porch, the ebbing tide gurgled. Mooring lights glistened across the water. On the float, the shack windows glimmered glassily with reflected light from the house. The porch creaked. Mike took a deep breath, walked to the door. It was unlocked. The knob made a clicking sound. He pushed.

"Holly?"

He let the sound of his voice go dead. Light glared over the sink. He leaned the door shut, resting his shoulders against it. He heard her call from the bedroom.

"Mike?"

"Yes."

"I'm in here."

The drum started beating. Holly. Holly. Holly... God in heaven, I love you. I love you, Holly. His eyes blurred. In the sink, a drop dripped from the faucet. Another drop formed. It fell, water beading metal. Jake's place. He was dead. You can't love a girl who had done what Herb said she had. But Herb was crazy. And I could love, I can, I do.

Mike clenched his fists. Another drop dripped. One drop, one day, one year, one life. All the same. Whatever you did was water dripping down a drain. Goodness was other folks' ideas of what you should do. To hell with them. Get on top of the heap. Fat Joe knew.

"Mike?"

"I'm coming, Holly."

She looked like an angel. In a soft, full nightgown, she sat on the bed. The lovely legs were crossed. Blond hair shimmered under the brush. Light glowed creamily along the smooth slant of cheek and graceful curve of neck.

Holly.

Mike waited. He filled himself with the vibrant warmth of her. Under the transparent nylon, her high breasts shaped nakedness. His thoughts snaked down, flame hot in his groin.

"Mike?"

"Yes, Holly."

"Like me?"

"Yes," he said. "I could never forget you, Holly. Not in a million years. No matter what ever happens to you."

"That's a funny thing to say, Mike."

He forced himself to smile. She made a place for him. He sat down. The silhouette of her body moved sinuously. She held her hair brush in her lap. He fumbled for his cigarettes. She shook her head, but he lit one for himself. After two puffs, he got up, squashing it out in the ashtray on the dresser. He came back to the bed and sat down. Closer to her.

"Holly."

"Yes?"

"Do you love me?"

She stared at him, and then, pushing away the brush, she turned. The nightgown hugged tightly across her thighs. She touched his hand. Her fingers were firm, untrembling.

"That's funny, too. A funny thing to ask." Her blue eyes, clear, looked into his. She pouted, and spoke huskily, "Mike, you've been gone a long time."

"Yes," he said stiffly.

"Is something wrong, Mike?"

He stared at her. Yes. He was sure. The promise still waited in her eyes.

Anything.

Just ask me.

He saw the beginning: that hot night, Ted and the old man playing cribbage. Yes, she was the same. Untouched. Like the water out there in the harbor. A man could drown. The water didn't care. It was just as beautiful as ever. Or, if you were afraid of it, just as ugly. She had the same unmarked serenity. The hot melting eyes offered the same promise.

His legs and arms felt wooden. Dryness ached in his throat. The lift of her slithered under the sheer nylon. He could have it all now, the smooth warmth of her legs, the golden slenderness surrendering. Emptiness sucked at his belly. Carla whispered at the rim of his mind. *Get out, Mike.* And Mig. *Stay, Mike…*

The bed creaked. Holly twisted closer. Her mouth was warm and red. Her hair was like golden honey. But Mike was with Herb in the darkness against the flat wall of the warehouse. Memory screamed the choking voice, the bugging eyes and Herb telling what he had seen. Jake fell. Water swirled. Mike licked his lips. Holly turned to him.

"Mike?"

He squeezed his eyes.

"Mike," she said again.

"Yes."

"You asked if I love you." Her arm lifted. She touched his hair, fondled it. Her gaze was wide and direct. "I do, Mike," she whispered. "I love you."

"You're a kid," he said to her. "You're just a kid."

"Mike, you're talking funny."

"Well, I had forgotten," Mike said. "I had stopped thinking of you as a kid." The stiffness had gone to his face. Words echoed in the tunnel of his mind. Out of shadows, he watched through his eyes. It was as if he saw too clearly, too much, the whole reel at once: ragged years, the old man drunk and vomiting his guts on the kitchen table, the wet dripping, the mud, junk, rottenness, fish stink, broken bottles. God, it was all there: the big-boat fishing, the hot sun and tuna thrashing a froth of blood, the publicity, Fat Joe, fights. And it all added up to this, this right here, in a room with Holly.

Years were chunks of life dropped in soft mud. Gone, every damned thing, gone old Jake and maybe Ted. None of it made a difference, either. Holly was still beautiful, and he listened to the echo of his jagged, hurting words: "Just a kid. I guess it doesn't mean anything. Why should it? Ted's in the hospital, Jake is dead. Everything belongs to you and Ted, maybe to you. That's a kick, isn't it? I mean, old Jake never got anything out of his money. He was like some damned pack rat. He just kept accumulating things. And old Jake got to be kind of rich, a dirty, stingy rich man, just looking out of his hole and stacking things up. Now you'll get it all, likely, and you're just a kid."

Holly moved away from him. "Funny talk, Mike."

He got up. He lit a cigarette and looked at her. "No," he said. "Not so funny. It all ought to be just the way we want it. You love me, you say. Right?"

"Yes," she whispered, puzzled. "That's right, Mike. I love you. I'd do anything you want."

"Anything?"

"Yes, Mike. Just ask me."

Time stopped. He breathed hard. She was looking at him, her eyes big with wonder. He kept talking, trying to put into words the way he felt. Something was wrong, he knew that, none of it was what he had meant to say; the things bothering him he could not put into words— but he kept talking. Looking at Holly, he knew she was all the woman he could ever want, all any man could ever want. But the words kept forming and coming out.

"Carla told me there was a man out there when Ted fell into the water. She could see him from his room. Herb Dean says there was a woman there when old Jake fell through the railing. He says the woman was you, and that you pushed him."

Holly uncoiled from the bed. Her eyes blazed. "I didn't do it, Mike."

"Were you there? Did you see it? All right, he wasn't pushed—he fell. Couldn't you have saved him?"

"Mike," she said softly, "I came down to your place to be with you. Could I have pushed the old man into the water and then made love? Could I have watched him drown and then come to you?"

"You wanted money more than anything in the world. You were always saying it."

"Mike—the old man was good to me. You're letting this get to you. Mike, don't look at me like that. I'm here now, waiting for you. Mike, it's me, Holly."

He knew he was glaring, looking at her as though he had never seen her before. The honey-blond—the warm, golden body—oh, desirable beyond any woman. But for the first time he was seeing beneath the soft curves of flesh, seeing the hardness inside, the greed, the cupidity.

"Yes, it's you, Holly," he said.

She knew, all of a sudden. She knew as surely as he did.

"You don't want me any more, is that it? You don't want me."

"Want you? I'll always want you," he said, certain it was the truth. And then he added, as truthfully, "But not the way you are. I'll want—I'll always want what I thought you were—what I thought we had."

"Mike—don't listen to them. I did no wrong."

"That's what I said. You didn't, you couldn't. But don't you see—the fact that I could think even for a minute that maybe you had..."

"All right." She tossed her head, hair blondly shimmering. "If that's what you want to think of me, forget it."

He took her in with his eyes as she stood there in her filmy nightgown. What a magnificent creature. And how dangerous. He had always heard there was a fine line between love and hate; now he understood. She leaned to recover the hairbrush from the bed. Her hand suddenly drew back. The hairbrush came sailing across the room at him.

He ducked easily, his fighter's reflexes always with him. The brush flew past, clattered on the wall, fell to the floor.

"Saying no to me," she stormed, "after what we risked together, what we shared!"

He regarded her mildly.

He was astonished at the way he felt, now that he saw Holly clearly, now that he was not blinded by love. He felt disappointed and drained, yet oddly relieved as though tons of dead weight had been lifted from his shoulders.

"Wasting my time on you, thinking you were something special," she railed. "I should have seen you were only another man, out for what you could get from me. I should have known it from the way you kept after those other two women. I'll tell you this much, Mike Shannon—I didn't kill old Jake and I didn't ambush Ted. All I wanted was you and money. Is that a sin?"

"No," he said, "and yes. You didn't kill them—but you wanted them dead, you wanted them out of the way. It isn't that I ever thought you actually bushwhacked them ..."

Her anger had left her. She stared. She was seeing him differently, too.

"I suppose I was guilty, in a way," she said. "I wanted you so much, and I wanted position and the things I'd never had. Yes, you're reading me right, Mike. In my heart I longed for them to die. Ted, because he stood between you and me. The old man, because he had the money."

He nodded. "You didn't harm them except by thinking, except by wishing them out of the way."

"Ted deserved death," she said. "Sitting around, drinking, taking all he could from the old man, never giving anything in return. But Jake—I liked the old man. I wouldn't have hurt him."

"Not even for his money?"

"Not even for his money," Holly said, and then sat down on the bed and started to cry, and she was a kid again. "Sure, I wanted his money. I wanted him out of the way, but that was only a matter of waiting. Meanwhile, I tried to help him, make him happy and comfortable. I got a kick out of it. It gave me a good feeling."

"All right, you've got his money now or Ted will have it, and you can wind him around your finger if you just play up to him a little."

"Ted's going to live," she said. "He was better today. I visited the hospital. He's come out of that long coma, even said a few words to the nurse." Her tears stopped. Mike could see that she was thinking hard. "You figure Herb Dean can cause me trouble? Why did he say what he did?"

"Herb is crazy," Mike answered. "He was out to make some deal with me, but I think he's caused all the trouble he's going to. You know, Monty Gomez said someone had been watching—he thought it had been me. It was Herb, of course. And it must have been Herb that Carla saw from her window."

"You see?" Holly said. "Everything will settle down and work out."

"Even me?" Mike asked.

"A girl can't have everything," Holly said. She was quiet, seemed at peace, as though she had come to some important adjustment. Mike was surprised at how easy it was to be in her presence now, to talk without passion, without tension.

"What do you expect to do?" he asked.

"I'm going to the hospital and start taking care of my husband," Holly said. "That's what I should have been doing all along, instead of staying here to see you."

"You had old Jake to take care of," Mike said. Now that the old man is gone, he thought, Ted is the one with the money. Of course you'll take care of him.

"Nothing for me to do here now," Holly said. "If Ted is beginning to get better, he'll need me."

Maybe that's the thing, he thought. Maybe she needs to be needed. Needed as a woman, a home-maker, a comforter—not as a girl with a lovely face and a body superior at sex.

"You go take care of him," Mike said. "See if you can make a man of him. Old Jake didn't do it—maybe you can. And maybe he can make a woman out of you."

She flushed, looked at him questioningly.

"There's more to being a woman than catching a man's eye and relieving him of his lust," he said. And having a cash register where your heart should be, he added silently. "Build his ego. Let him think you think he's just fine—even between the sheets. Yes, you go take care of Ted. I'll take care of the dock for a while."

It turned out to be quite a while.

Ted gradually improved, after a while he was able to answer questions. Monty Gomez paid another visit to Mike, not appearing nearly as ominous.

"We had to send Herb Dean away," Monty said, sucking a toothpick. "He's always been a little screwy, but now he's clean off his rocker. Was saying something about you threatening him. Said he saw Mrs. Adam kill old Jake and before that she tried to kill Ted. But the old man evidently fell through that bad spot in the railing —and Ted says no one hit him, he slipped, banged his head on a rock. He was pretty drunk, but he can remember it. And it was confirmed by Herb. He happened to be on the path at the time, but said nothing for two reasons, one crazier than the other. First, he hates cops. Second, he was afraid he would be accused of having attacked Ted." Monty spat out the toothpick. "What are you going to do now, Mike?"

"I'll see," Mike said. A couple of days later he stopped in at the hospital and decided. Ted, looking peaked but alert, was propped up in bed.

"The old man always wanted me to go to school," Ted said. "If you'd like to stay here and run the business, Holly and I will take off for the big city."

"To study?" Mike asked.

"This time to study," Ted said. "I guess that's the least I can do for the old man. I've had my lesson."

"And what's the lesson?"

"Life is short, and it's frail. You have to move fast to grab it, and handle it easy or it will break. I'll tell you something, I never appreciated Holly. I heard she was good to the old man. She's being real good to me."

Mike reported the gist of the conversation to Mig, walking along the beach as they so often did lately.

"Maybe he is growing up," Mig said. "We all have things to face. Ted has to face the fact that he isn't much of a man. Maybe he figures some education will make him one. It can't, by itself. But buckling down and working—that might do it."

"I thought I was the philosopher," Mike said.

"It's catching," Mig said. "My philosophy now is that every day, life starts all over again."

"Can you believe that for us, Mig?"

"Can you?"

He knew the answer. The circle closed, the end with the beginning.

"Can you?" Mig asked again.

"Yes," he said, "I can. If you don't run out of new colors for your hair."

He bent down, kissing her mouth. Then she lifted herself, clinging, her arms going around his neck. He said words softly against the trembling warmth of her lips, softly because they came from deep inside him.

"I'm home now, Mig. This time, I'm really home."

"Maybe. But you'll soon be leaving."

"I will?"

"That's right. I'm going with you. We've got to help Carla. She voluntarily gave that newspaper the whole story of Fat Joe's operations."

"I know she did. Supplied proof, too. That's the end of Joe."

"Sure, but did you listen to the radio reports this morning? Joe managed to get her arrested on an old murder charge. She's going to need friends, money."

"We can be her friends. I don't know about money," said Mike.

Mig laughed.

"I've got enough money to hire ten lawyers for her. Herb's father was one of the original cannery people, you know. Herb was even stingier than old Jake, but now that the poor guy is in an institution, the court has awarded me the whole estate." She took his hand. "Of course, I don't even know the woman. And you came straight out of her bed into mine—that's why we didn't exactly light a bonfire that night, I figure. But she did stand up to Fat Joe. She got revenge for you."

She started to trudge across the sand, tugging him along by the hand.

"Mig?"

"Yes?"

"Wait a minute." He wanted to kiss her. He did. A diesel trawler chugged. Waves crested, spilling the water into the slough. Along the highway, a fish truck shifted gears for the grade below the bridge. And Mike kissed Mig.

THE END

www.ingramcontent.com/pod-product-compliance
Lightning Source LLC
Chambersburg PA
CBHW030344180626
46812CB00007B/2756

* 9 7 8 1 9 5 2 1 3 8 9 5 9 *